Soldiers Thr

(Part 2)

Rudyard Kipling

Alpha Editions

This edition published in 2023

ISBN : 9789357963343

Design and Setting By
Alpha Editions
www.alphaedis.com
Email - info@alphaedis.com

Contents

'LOVE-O'WOMEN'

A lamentable tale of things

Done long ago, and ill done.

The horror, the confusion, and the separation of the murderer from his comrades were all over before I came. There remained only on the barrack-square the blood of man calling from the ground. The hot sun had dried it to a dusky gold-beater-skin film, cracked lozenge-wise by the heat, and as the wind rose each lozenge, rising a little, curled up at the edges as if it were a dumb tongue. Then a heavier gust blew all away down wind in grains of dark-coloured dust. It was too hot to stand in the sunshine before breakfast. The men were all in barracks talking the matter over. A knot of soldiers' wives stood by one of the entrances to the married quarters, while inside a woman shrieked and raved with wicked filthy words.

A quiet and well-conducted sergeant had shot down in broad daylight just after early parade one of his own corporals, had then returned to barracks and sat on a cot till the guard came for him. He would, therefore, in due time be handed over to the High Court for trial. Further, but this he could hardly have considered in his scheme of revenge, he would horribly upset my work; for the reporting of the trial would fall on me without a relief. What that trial would be like I knew even to weariness. There would be the rifle carefully uncleaned, with the fouling marks about breech and muzzle, to be sworn to by half a dozen superfluous privates; there would be heat, reeking heat, till the wet pencil slipped sideways between the fingers; and the punkah would swish and the pleaders would jabber in the verandahs, and his Commanding Officer would put in certificates of the prisoner's moral character, while the jury would pant and the summer uniforms of the witnesses would smell of dye and soaps; and some abject barrack-sweeper would lose his head in cross-examination, and the young barrister who always defended soldiers' cases for the credit that they never brought him, would say and do wonderful things, and would then quarrel with me because I had not reported him correctly. At the last, for he surely would not be hanged, I might meet the prisoner again, ruling blank account-forms in the Central Jail, and cheer him with the hope of a wardership in the Andamans.

The Indian Penal Code and its interpreters do not treat murder, under any provocation whatever, in a spirit of jest. Sergeant Raines would be very lucky indeed if he got off with seven years, I thought. He had slept the night upon his wrongs, and had killed his man at twenty yards before any talk was possible. That much I knew. Unless, therefore, the case was doctored a little, seven years would be his least; and I fancied it was exceedingly well for Sergeant Raines that he had been liked by his Company.

That same evening—no day is so long as the day of a murder—I met Ortheris with the dogs, and he plunged defiantly into the middle of the matter. "I'll be one o' the witnesses," said he. "I was in the verandah when Mackie came along. 'E come from Mrs. Raines's quarters. Quigley, Parsons, an' Trot, they was in the inside verandah, so they couldn't 'ave 'eard nothing. Sergeant Raines was in the verandah talkin' to me, an' Mackie 'e come along acrost the square an' 'e sez, 'Well,' sez 'e, "ave they pushed your 'elmet off yet, Sergeant?' 'e sez. An' at that Raines 'e catches 'is breath an' 'e sez, 'My Gawd, I can't stand this!' sez 'e, an' 'e picks up my rifle an' shoots Mackie. See?"

"But what were you doing with your rifle in the outer verandah an hour after parade?"

"Cleanin' 'er," said Ortheris, with the sullen brassy stare that always went with his choice lies.

He might as well have said that he was dancing naked, for at no time did his rifle need hand or rag on her twenty minutes after parade. Still the High Court would not know his routine.

"Are you going to stick to that—on the Book?" I asked.

"Yes. Like a bloomin' leech."

"All right, I don't want to know any more. Only remember that Quigley, Parsons, and Trot couldn't have been where you say without hearing something; and there's nearly certain to be a barrack-sweeper who was knocking about the square at the time. There always is."

"Twasn't the sweeper. It was the beastie. 'E's all right."

Then I knew that there was going to be some spirited doctoring, and I felt sorry for the Government Advocate who would conduct the prosecution.

When the trial came on I pitied him more, for he was always quick to lose his temper, and made a personal matter of each lost cause. Raines's young barrister had for once put aside his unslaked and Welling passion for alibis and insanity, had forsworn gymnastics and fireworks, and worked soberly for his client. Mercifully the hot weather was yet young, and there had been no flagrant cases of barrack-shootings up to the time; and the jury was a good one, even for an Indian jury, where nine men out of every twelve are accustomed to weighing evidence. Ortheris stood firm and was not shaken by any cross-examination. The one weak point in his tale—the presence of his rifle in the outer verandah—went unchallenged by civilian wisdom, though some of the witnesses could not help smiling. The Government Advocate called for the rope; contending throughout that the murder had been a deliberate one. Time had passed, he argued, for that reflection which comes so naturally to a man whose honour is lost. There was also the Law, ever ready and anxious to right the wrongs of the common soldier if, in deed, wrong had been done. But he doubted much whether there had been any sufficient wrong. Causeless suspicion over-long brooded upon had led, by his theory, to deliberate crime. But his attempts to minimise the motive failed. The most disconnected witness knew—had known for weeks—the causes of offence, and the prisoner, who naturally was the last of all to know, groaned in the dock while he listened. The one question that the trial circled round was whether Raines had fired under sudden and blinding provocation given that very morning, and in the summing up it was clear that Ortheris's evidence told. He had contrived, most artistically, to suggest that he personally hated the Sergeant, who had come into the verandah to give him a talking to for insubordination. In a weak moment the Government Advocate asked one question too many, "Beggin' your pardon, sir," Ortheris replied, "'e was callin' me a dam' impudent little lawyer." The Court shook. The jury brought it in a killing, but with every provocation and extenuation known to God or man, and the Judge put his hand to his brow before giving sentence, and the Adam's apple in the prisoner's throat went up and down mercury-pumping before a cyclone.

In consideration of all considerations, from his Commanding Officer's certificate of good conduct to the sure loss of pension, service, and honour, the prisoner would get two years, to be served in India, and—there need be no demonstration in Court. The Government Advocate scowled and picked up his papers; the guard wheeled with a clash, and the prisoner was relaxed to the Secular Arm, and driven to the jail in a broken-down ticca-gharri.

His guard and some ten or twelve military witnesses, being less important, were ordered to wait till what was officially called the cool of the evening before marching back to cantonments. They gathered together in one of the deep red brick verandahs of a disused lock-up and congratulated Ortheris, who bore his honours modestly. I sent my work into the office and joined them. Ortheris watched the Government Advocate driving off lunch.

"That's a nasty little bald-'eaded little butcher, that is," he said. "'E don't please me. 'E's got a colley dog wot do, though. I'm goin' up to Murree in a week. That dawg'll bring fifteen rupees anywheres."

"You had better spend it in Masses," said Terence, unbuckling his belt, for he had been on the prisoner's guard, standing helmeted and bolt up right for three long hours.

"Not me," said Ortheris cheerfully. "Gawd'll put it down to B Comp'ny's barrick damages one o' these days. You look strapped, Terence."

"Faith, I'm not so young as I was. That guard-mountin' wears on the sole av the fut, and this"—he sniffed contemptuously at the brick verandah—"is as hard setting as standin'!"

"Wait a minute. I'll get the cushions out of my cart," I said.

"Strewth—sofies! We're going it gay," said Ortheris, as Terence dropped himself section by section on the leather cushions, saying prettily, "May you niver want a soft place wheriver you go, an' power to share utt wid a frind. Another for yourself? That's good. It lets me sit long ways. Stanley, pass me a poipe. Augrrh! An' that's another man gone all to pieces bekaze av a woman. I must ha' been on forty or fifty prisoners' gyards, first an' last, an' I hate ut new ivry time."

"Let's see. You were on Losson's, Lancey's, Dugard's, and Stebbins's, that I can remember," I said.

"Ay, an' before that an' before that—scores av thim," he answered with a worn smile. "'Tis betther to die than to live for thim, though. Whin Raines comes out—he'll be changin' his kit at the jail now—he'll think that too. He shud ha' shot himself an' the woman by rights, an' made a clean bill av all. Now he's left the woman—she tuk tay wid Dinah Sunday gone last—an' he's left himself. Mackie's the lucky man."

"He's probably getting it hot where he is," I ventured, for I knew something of the dead Corporal's record.

"Be sure av that," said Terence, spitting over the edge of the verandah. "But fwhat he'll get there is light marchin'-ordher to fwhat he'd ha' got here if he'd lived."

"Surely not. He'd have gone on and forgotten like the others."

"Did ye know Mackie well, Sorr?" said Terence.

"He was on the Pattiala guard of honour last winter, and I went out shooting with him in an ekka for the day, and I found him rather an amusing man."

"Well, he'll ha' got shut av amusemints, excipt turnin' from wan side to the other, these few years come. I knew Mackie, an' I've seen too many to be mistuk in the muster av wan man. He might ha' gone on an' forgot, as you say, Sorr, but was a man wid an educashin, an' he used ut for his schames, an' the same educashin, an' talk an' all that made him able to do fwhat he had a mind to wid a woman, that same wud turn back again in the long run an' tear him alive. I can't say fwhat that I mane to say bekaze I don't know how, but Mackie was the spit an' livin' image av a man that I saw march the same march all but; an' 'twas worse for him that he did not come by Mackie's ind. Wait while I remimber now. 'Twas fwhin I was in the Black Tyrone, an' he was drafted us from Portsmouth; an' fwhat was his misbegotten name? Larry—Larry Tighe ut was; an' wan of the draft said he was a gentleman ranker, an' Larry tuk an' three parts killed him for saying so. An' he was a big man, an' a strong man, an' a handsome man, an' that tells heavy in practice wid some women, but, takin' thim by an' large, not wid all. Yet 'twas wid all that Larry dealt—all—for he 'ud put the comether on any woman that trod the green earth av God, an' he knew ut. Like Mackie that's roastin' now, he knew ut; an' niver did he put the comether on any woman save an' excipt for the black shame. 'Tis not me that shud be talkin', dear knows, dear knows, but the most av my mis—misalli'nces was for pure devilry, an' mighty sorry I have been whin harm came; an' time an' again wid a girl, ay, an' a woman too, for the matter av that, whin I have seen by the eyes av her that I was makin' more throuble than I talked, I have hild off an' let be for the sake av the mother that bore me. But Larry, I'm thinkin', he was suckled by a she-devil, for he niver let wan go that came nigh to listen to him. 'Twas his business, as if it might ha' bin sinthry-go. He was a good soldier too. Now there was the Colonel's governess—an' he a privit too!—that was never known in barricks; an' wan av the Major's maids, and she was promised to a man; an' some more outside; an' fwhat ut was amongst us we'll never know till Judgment Day! 'Twas the nature av the baste to put the comether on the best av thim—not the prettiest by any manner av manes—but the like av such woman as you cud lay your band on the Book an' swear there was niver thought av foolishness in. An' for that very reason, mark you, he was niver caught. He came close to ut wanst or twice, but caught he niver was, an' that cost him more at the ind than the beginnin'. He talked to me more than most, bekaze he tould me, barrin' the accident av my educashin, I'd ha' been the same kind av divil he was. 'An' is ut like,' he wud say, houldin' his head high—'is ut like that I'd iver be thrapped? For fwhat am I when all's said an' done?' he sez. 'A damned privit,' sez he. 'An' is ut like, think you, that thim I know wud be connect wid a privit like me? Number tin thousand four hundred an' sivin,' he sez, grinnin'. I knew by the turn av his spache whin he was not takin' care to talk rough that he was a gentleman ranker.

"'I do not undherstan' ut at all,' I sez; 'but I know,' sez I, 'that the divil looks out av your eyes, an' I'll have no share wid you. A little fun by way av amusemint where 't will do no harm, Larry, is right and fair, but I am mistook if 'tis any amusemint to you,' I sez.

"'You are much mistook,' he sez. 'An' I counsel you not to judge your betters.'

"'My betthers!' I sez. 'God help you, Larry. There's no betther in this. 'Tis all bad, as you will find for yoursilf.'

"You're not like me,' he says, tossin' his head.

"'Praise the Saints, I am not,' I sez. 'Fwhat I have done I have done an' been crool sorry for. Fwhin your time comes,' sez I, 'ye'll remimber fwhat I say.'

"'An' whin that time comes,' sez he, 'I'll come to you for ghostly consolation, Father Terence,' an' at that he wint off afther some more divil's business—for to get expayrience, he tould me. He was wicked—rank wicked—wicked as all Hell! I'm not construct by nature to go in fear av any man, but, begad, I was afraid av Larry. He'd come in to barricks wid his cap on three hairs, an' lie on his cot and stare at the ceilin', and now an' again he'd fetch a little laugh, the like av a splash in the bottom av a well, an' by that I knew he was schamin' new wickedness, an' I'd be afraid. All this was long an' long ago, but ut hild me straight—for a while.

"I tould you, did I not, Sorr, that I was caressed an' pershuaded to lave the Tyrone on account av a throuble?"

"Something to do with a belt and a man's head, wasn't it?" Terence had never given me the exact facts.

"It was. Faith, ivry time I go on prisoner's gyard in coort I wondher fwhy I am not where the pris'ner is. But the man I struk tuk it in fair fight, an' he had the good sinse not to die. Considher now, fwhat wud ha' come to the Arrmy if he had! I was enthreated to exchange, an' my Commandin' Orf'cer pled wid me. I wint, not to be disobligin', an' Larry tould me he was powerful sorry to lose me, though fwhat I'd done to make him sorry I do not know. So to the Ould Rig'mint I came, lavin' Larry to go to the divil his own way, an' niver expectin' to see him again except as a shootin'-case in barricks.... Who's that lavin' the compound?" Terence's quick eye had caught sight of a white uniform skulking behind hedge.

"The Sergeant's gone visiting," said a voice.

"Thin I command here, an' I will have no sneakin' away to the bazar, an' huntin' for you wid a pathrol at midnight. Nalson, for I know ut's you, come back to the verandah."

Nalson, detected, slunk back to his fellows. There was a grumble that died away in a minute or two, and Terence, turning on the other side, went on:—

"That was the last I saw av Larry for a while. Exchange is the same as death for not thinkin', an' by token I married Dinah, an' that kept me from remimberin' ould times. Thin we wint up to the Front, an' ut tore my heart in tu to lave Dinah at the Depot in Pindi. Consequint whin was at the Front I fought circumspectuous till I warrmed up, an thin I fought double tides. You remimber fwhat I tould you in the gyard-gate av the fight at Silver's Theatre."

"Wot's that about Silver's Theayter!" said Ortheris quickly, over his shoulder.

"Nothin', little man. A tale that ye know. As I was sayin', afther that fight us av the Ould Rig'mint an' the Tyrone was all mixed together takin' shtock ay the dead, an' av coorse I wint about to find if there was any man that remimbered me. The second man I came acrost—an' how I'd missed him in the fight I do not know—was Larry, an' a fine man he looked, but oulder, by token that he had a call to be. 'Larry,' sez I, 'how is ut wid you?'

"'Ye're callin' the wrong man,' he sez, wid his gentleman's smile; 'Larry has been dead these three years. They call him "Love-o'-Women" now,' he sez. By that I knew the ould divil was in him yet, but the ind av a fight is no time for the beginnin' av confession, so we sat down an' talked av times.'

"'They tell me you're a married man,' he sez, puffing slow at his poipe. 'Are ye happy?'

"'I will be whin I get back to Depot,' I sez. "Tis a reconnaissance honeymoon now.'

"'I'm married too,' he sez, puffin' slow an' more slow, an' stopperin' wid his forefinger.

"'Sind you happiness,' I sez. 'That's the best hearin' for a long time.'

"'Are ye av that opinion?' he sez; an' thin he began talkin' av the campaign. The sweat av Silver's Theatre was not dhry upon him, an' he was prayin' for more work. I was well contint to lie and listen to the cook-pot lids.

"Whin he got up off the ground he shtaggered a little, an' laned over all twisted.

"'Ye've got more than ye bargained for,' I sez. 'Take an inventory, Larry. 'Tis like you're hurt.'

"He turned round stiff as a ramrod an' damned the eyes av me up an' down for an impartinent Irish-faced ape. If that had been in barricks, I'd ha' stretched him an' no more said; but 'twas at the Front, an' afther such a fight as Silver's Theatre I knew there was no callin' a man to account for his timpers. He might as well ha' kissed me. Aftharwards I was well pleased I kept my fistes home. Then our Captain Crook—Cruik-na-bul-leen—came up. He'd been talkin' to the little orf'cer bhoy av the Tyrone. 'We're all cut to windystraws,' he sez, 'but the Tyrone are damned short for noncoms. Go you over there, Mulvaney, an' be Deputy-Sergeant, Corp'ral, Lance, an' everything else ye can lay hands on till I bid you stop.'

"'I wint over an' tuk hould. There was wan sergeant left standin', an' they'd pay no heed to him. The remnint was me, an' 'twas high time I came. Some I talked to, an' some I did not, but before night the bhoys av the Tyrone stud to attention, begad, if I sucked on my poipe above a whishper. Betune you an' me an' Bobs, I was commandin' the company, an' that was what Cruik had thransferred me for, an' the little orf'cer bhoy knew ut, and I knew ut, but the comp'ny did not. And there, mark you, is the vartue that no money an' no dhrill can buy—the vartue av the ould soldier that knows his orf'cer's work an' does ut—at the salute!

"Thin the Tyrone, wid the Ould Rig'mint in touch, was sint maraudin' and prowlin' acrost the hills promishcuous an' unsatisfactory. 'Tis my privit opinion that a gin'ral does not know half his time fwhat to do wid three-quarthers his command. So he shquats on his hunkers an' bids thim run round an' round forninst him while he considhers on ut. Whin by the process av nature they get sejuced into a big fight that was none av their seekin', he sez: 'Obsarve my shuparior janius! I meant ut to come so.' We ran round an' about, an' all we got was shootin' into the camp at night, an' rushin' empty sungars wid the long bradawl, an' bein' hit from behind rocks till we was wore out—all except Love-o'-Women. That puppy-dog business was mate an' dhrink to him. Begad, he cud niver get enough av ut. Me well knowin' that it is just this desultorial campaignin' that kills the best men, an' suspicionin' that if I was cut the little orf'cer bhoy wud expind all his men in thryin' to get out, I wud lie most powerful doggo whin I heard a shot, an' curl my long legs behind a bowlder, an' run like blazes whin the ground was clear. Faith, if I led the Tyrone in rethreat wanst I led them forty times. Love-o'-Women wud stay pottin' an' pottin' from behind a rock, and wait till the fire was heaviest, an' thin stand up an' fire man-height clear. He wud lie out in camp too at night snipin' at the shadows, for he niver tuk a mouthful av slape. My commandin' orf'cer—save his little soul!—cud not see the beauty av of my strategims, an' whin the Ould Rig'mint crossed us, an' that was wanst a week, he'd throt off to Cruik, wid his big blue eyes as round as saucers, an' lay an information against me. I heard thim wanst talkin' through the tent-wall, an' I nearly laughed.

"'He runs—runs like a hare,' sez the little orf'cer bhoy. ''Tis demoralisin' my men.'

"'Ye damned little fool,' sez Cruik, laughin'. 'He's larnin' you your business. Have ye been rushed at night yet?'

"'No,' sez the child, wishful that he had been.

"'Have you any wounded?' sez Cruik.

"'No,' he sez. 'There was no chanst for that. They follow Mulvaney too quick,' he sez.

"'Fwhat more do you want, thin?' sez Cruik. 'Terence is bloodin' you neat an' handy,' he sez. 'He knows fwhat you do not, an' that's that there's a time for ivrything. He'll not lead you wrong,' he sez, 'but I'd give a month's pay to larn fwhat he thinks av you.'

"That kept the babe quiet, but Love-o'-Women was pokin' at me for ivrything I did, an' specially my manoeuvres.

"'Mr. Mulvaney,' he sez wan evenin', very contempshus, 'you're growin' very jeldy wid your feet. Among gentlemen,' he sez, 'among gentlemen that's called no pretty name.'

"'Among privits 'tis different,' I sez. 'Get back to your tent. I'm sergeant here,' I sez.

"There was just enough in the voice av me to tell him he was playin' wid his life betune his teeth. He wint off, an' I noticed that this man that was contempshus set off from the halt wid a shunt as tho' he was bein' kicked behind. That same night there was a Paythan picnic in the hills about, an' firin' into our tents fit to wake the livin' dead. 'Lie down all,' I sez. 'Lie down an' kape still. They'll no more than waste ammunition.'

"I heard a man's feet on the ground, an' thin a 'Tini joinin' in the chorus. I'd been lyin' warm, thinkin' av Dinah an' all, but I crup out wid the bugle for to look round in case there was a rush, an' the 'Tini was flashin' at the fore-ind av the camp, an' the hill near by was fair flickerin' wid long-range fire. Undher the starlight I beheld Love-o'-Women settin' on a rock wid his belt and helmet off. He shouted wanst or twice, an' thin I heard him say: 'They should ha' got the range long ago. Maybe they'll fire at the flash.' Thin he fired again, an' that dhrew a fresh volley, and the long slugs that they chew in their teeth came floppin' among the rocks like tree-toads av a hot night. 'That's better,' sez Love-o'-Women. 'Oh Lord, how long, how long!' he sez, an' at that he lit a match an' held ut above his head.

"'Mad,' thinks I, 'mad as a coot,' an' I tuk wan stip forward, an' the nixt I knew was the sole av my boot flappin' like a cavalry gydon an' the funny-bone av my toes tinglin'. 'Twas a clane-cut shot—a slug—that niver touched sock or hide, but set me bare-fut on the rocks. At that I tuk Love-o'-Women by the scruff an' threw him under a bowlder, an' whin I sat down I heard the bullets patterin' on that good stone.

"'Ye may dhraw your own wicked fire,' I sez, shakin' him, 'but I'm not goin' to be kilt too.'

"'Ye've come too soon,' he sez. 'Ye've come too soon. In another minute they cud not ha' missed me. Mother av God,' he sez, 'fwhy did ye not lave me be? Now 'tis all to do again,' an' he hides his face in his hands.

"'So that's it,' I sez, shakin' him again. 'That's th manin' av your disobeyin' ordhers.'

"'I dare not kill meself,' he sez, rockin' to and fro. 'My own hand wud not let me die, and there's not a bullet this month past wud touch me. I'm to die slow,' he sez. 'I'm to die slow. But I'm in hell now,' he sez, shriekin' like a woman. 'I'm in hell now!'

"'God be good to us all,' I sez, for I saw his face. 'Will ye tell a man the throuble. If 'tis not murder, maybe we'll mend it yet.'

"At that he laughed. 'D'you remimber fwhat I said in the Tyrone barricks about comin' to you for ghostly consolation. I have not forgot,' he sez. 'That came back, an' the rest av my time is on me now, Terence. I've fought ut off for months an' months, but the liquor will not bite any more, Terence,' he sez. 'I can't get dhrunk.'

"Thin I knew he spoke the truth about bein' in hell, for whin liquor does not take hould, the sowl av a man is rotten in him. But me bein' such as I was, fwhat could I say to him?

"'Di'monds an' pearls,' he begins again. 'Di'monds and pearls I have thrown away wid both hands—an' fwhat have I left? Oh, fwhat have I left?'

"He was shakin' an' thremblin' up against my shouldher, an' the slugs was singin' overhead, an' I was wonderin' whether my little bhoy wud have sinse enough to kape his men quiet through all this firin'.

"'So long as I did not think,' sez Love-o'-Women, 'so long I did not see—I wud not see—but I can now, what I've lost. The time an' the place,' he sez, 'an' the very words I said whin ut pleased me to go off alone to hell. But thin, even thin,' he sez, wrigglin' tremenjus, 'I wud not ha' been happy. There was too much behind av me. How cud I ha' believed her sworn oath—me that have bruk mine again an' again for the sport av seein' thim cry. An' there are the others,' he sez. 'Oh, what will I do—what will I do'?' He rocked back an' forward again, an' I think he was cryin' like wan av the women he dealt wid.

"The full half av fwhat he said was Brigade Ordhers to me, but from the rest an' the remnint I suspicioned somethin' av his throuble. 'Twas the judgmint av God had grup the heel av him, as I tould him 'twould in the Tyrone barricks. The slugs was singin' over our rock more an' more, an' I sez for to divart him: 'Let bad alone,' I sez. 'They'll be thryin' to rush the camp in a minut'.'

"I had no more than said that whin a Paythan man crep' up on his belly wid his knife betune his teeth, not twinty yards from us. Love-o'-Women jumped up an' fetched a yell, an' the man saw him an' ran at him (he'd left his rifle under the rock) wid the knife. Love-o'-Women niver turned a hair, but by the Living Power, for I saw ut, a stone twisted under the Paythan man's feet an' he came down full sprawl, an' his knife wint tinklin' acrost the rocks! 'I tould you I was Cain,' sez Love-o'-Women. 'Fwhat's the use av killin' him? He's an honest man—by compare.'

"I was not dishputin' about the morils av Paythans that tide, so I dhropped Love-o'-Women's burt acrost the man's face, an' 'Hurry into camp,' I sez, 'for this may be the first av a rush.'

"There was no rush afther all, though we waited undher arms to give thim a chanst. The Paythan man must ha' come alone for the mischief, an' afther a while Love-o'-Women wint back to his tint wid that quare lurchin' sind-off in his walk that I cud niver undherstand. Begad, I pitied him, an' the more bekaze he made me think for the rest av the night av the day whin I was confirmed Corp'ril, not actin' Lef'tenant, an' my thoughts was not good.

"Ye can undherstand that afther that night we came to talkin' a dale together, an' bit by bit ut came out fwhat I'd suspicioned. The whole av his carr'in's on an' divilmints had come back on him hard as liquor comes back whin you've been on the dhrink for a wake. All he'd said an' all he'd done, an' only he cud tell how much that was, come back, an' there was niver a minut's peace in his sowl. 'Twas the Horrors widout any cause to see, an' yet, an' yet—fwhat am I talkin' av? He'd ha' taken the Horrors wid thankfulness. Beyon' the repentince av the man, an' that was beyon' the natur av man—awful, awful, to behould!—there was more that was worst than any repentince. Av the scores an' scores that he called over in his mind (an' they were dhrivin' him mad), there was, mark you, wan woman av all, an' she was not his wife, that cut him to the quick av his marrow. 'Twas there he said that he'd thrown away di'monds an' pearls past count, an' thin he'd begin again like a blind byle in an oil-mill, walkin' round an' round, to considher (him that was beyond all touch av being happy this side hell!) how happy he wud ha' been wid her. The more he considhered, the more he'd consate himself that he'd lost mighty happiness, an' thin he wud work ut all backwards, an' cry that he niver cud ha' been happy anyways.

"Time an' time an' again in camp, on p'rade, ay, an' in action, I've seen that man shut his eyes an' duck his head as you wud duck to the flicker av a bay'nit. For 'twas thin he tould me that the thought av all he'd missed came an' stud forninst him like red-hot irons. For what he'd done wid the others he was sorry, but he did not care; but this wan woman that I've tould of, by the Hilts av God she made him pay for all the others twice over! Niver did I know that a man cud enjure such tormint widout his heart crackin' in his ribs, an' I have been"—Terence turned the pipe-stem slowly between his teeth—"I have been in some black cells. All I iver suffered tho' was not to be talked of alongside av him... an' what could I do? Paternosters was no more than peas for his sorrow.

"Evenshually we finished our prom'nade acrost the hills, and thanks to me for the same, there was no casualties an' no glory. The campaign was comin' to an ind, an' all the rig'mints was bein' drawn together for to be sint back home. Love-o'-Women was mighty sorry bekaze he had no work to do, an' all his time to think in. I've heard that man talkin' to his belt-plate an' his side-arms while he was soldierin' thim, all to prevint himself from thinkin', an' ivry time he got up afther he had been settin' down or wint on from the halt, he'd start wid that kick an' traverse that I tould you of—his legs sprawlin' all ways to wanst. He wud niver go see the docthor, tho' I tould him to be wise. He'd curse me up an' down for my advice; but I knew he was no more a man to be reckoned wid than the little bhoy was a commandin' orf'cer, so I let his tongue run if it aised him.

"Wan day—'twas on the way back—I was walkin' round camp wid him, an' he stopped an' struck ground wid his right fut three or four times doubtful. 'Fwhat is ut?' I sez. 'Is that ground?' sez he; an' while I was thinkin' his mind was goin', up comes the docthor, who'd been anatomisin' a dead bullock. Love-o'-Women starts to go on quick, an' lands me a kick on the knee while his legs was gettin' into marchin' ordher.

"'Hould on there,' sez the docthor; an' Love-o'-Women's face, that was lined like a gridiron, turns red as brick.

"''Tention,' says the docthor; an' Love-o'-Women stud so. 'Now shut your eyes,' sez the docthor. 'No, ye must not hould by your comrade.'

"''Tis all up,' sez Love-o'-Women, trying to smile. 'I'd fall, docthor, an' you know ut.'

"'Fall?' I sez. 'Fall at attention wid your eyes shut! Fwhat do you mane?'

"The docthor knows,' he sez. 'I've hild up as long as I can, but begad I'm glad 'tis all done. But I will die slow,' he sez, 'I will die very slow.'

"I cud see by the docthor's face that he was mortial sorry for the man, an' he ordhered him to hospital. We wint back together, an' I was dumbstruck; Love-o'-Women was cripplin' and crumblin' at ivry step. He walked wid a hand on my shoulder all slued sideways, an' his right leg swingin' like a lame camel. Me not knowin' more than the dead fwhat ailed him, 'twas just as though the docthor's word had done ut all—as if Love-o'-Women had but been waitin' for the ordher to let go.

"In hospital he sez somethin' to the docthor that I could not catch.

"'Holy shmoke!' sez the docthor, 'an' who are you to be givin' names to your diseases? 'Tis ag'in' all the regulations.'

"'I'll not be a privit much longer,' sez Love-o'-Women in his gentleman's voice, an' the docthor jumped.

"'Thrate me as a study, Docthor Lowndes,' he sez; an' that was the first time I'd iver heard a docthor called his name.

"'Good-bye, Terence,' sez Love-o'-Women. "Tis a dead man I am widout the pleasure av dyin'. You'll come an' set wid me sometimes for the peace av my soul.'

"Now I had been minded to ask Cruik to take me back to the Ould Rig'mint, for the fightin' was over, an' I was wore out wid the ways av the bhoys in the Tyrone; but I shifted my will, an' hild on, an' wint to set wid Love-o'-Women in the hospital. As I have said, Sorr, the man bruk all to little pieces undher my hand. How long he had hild up an' forced himself fit to march I cannot tell, but in hospital but two days later he was such as I hardly knew. I shuk hands wid him, an' his grip was fair strong, but his hands wint all ways to wanst, an' he cud not button his tunic.

"'I'll take long an' long to die yet,' he sez, 'for the ways av sin they're like interest in the rig'mintal savin's-bank—sure, but a damned long time bein' paid.'

"The docthor sez to me quiet one day, 'Has Tighe there anythin' on his mind?' he sez. 'He's burnin' himself out.'

"'How shud I know, Sorr?' I sez, as innocent as putty.

"'They call him Love-o'-Women in the Tyrone, do they not?' he sez. 'I was a fool to ask. Be wid him all you can. He's houldin' on to your strength.'

"'But what ails him, docthor,' I sez.

"'They call ut Locomotus attacks us,' he sez, 'bekaze,' sez he, 'ut attacks us like a locomotive, if ye know fwhat that manes. An' ut comes,' sez he, lookin' at me, 'ut comes from bein' called Love-o'-Women.'

"'You're jokin', docthor,' I sez.

"'Jokin'!' sez he. 'If iver you feel that you've got a felt sole in your boot instead av a Government bull's-wool, come to me,' he sez, 'an' I'll show you whether 'tis a joke.'

"You would not belave ut, Sorr, but that an' seein' Love-o'-Women overtuk widout warnin' put the cowld fear av attacks us on me so strong that for a week an' more I was kickin' my toes against stones an' stumps for the pleasure av feelin' them hurt.

"An' Love-o'-Women lay in the cot (he might have gone down wid the wounded before an' before, but he asked to stay wid me), and fwhat there was in his mind had full swing at him night an' day an' ivry hour av the day an' the night, an' he withered like beef rations in a hot sun, an' his eyes was like owls' eyes, an' his hands was mut'nous.

"They was gettin' the rig'mints away wan by wan, the campaign bein' inded, but as ushuil they was behavin' as if niver a rig'mint had been moved before in the mem'ry av man. Now, fwhy is that, Sorr? There's fightin' in an' out nine months av the twelve somewhere in the Army. There has been—for years an' years an' years, an' I wud ha' thought they'd begin to get the hang av providin' for throops. But no! Ivry time it's like a girls' school meetin' a big red bull whin they're goin' to church; an' 'Mother av God,' sez the Commissariat an' the railways an' the Barrick-masters, 'fwhat will we do now?' The ordhers came to us av the Tyrone an' the Ould Rig'mint an' half a dozen more to go down, and there the ordhers stopped dumb. We wint down, by the special grace av God—down the Khaiber anyways. There was sick wid us, an' I'm thinkin' that some av them was jolted to death in the doolies, but they was anxious to be kilt so if they cud get to Peshawur alive the sooner. I walked by Love-o'-Women—there was no marchin', an' Love-o'-Women was not in a stew to get on. 'If I'd only ha' died up there!' sez he through the doolie-curtains, an' then he'd twist up his eyes an' duck his head for the thoughts that came to him.

"Dinah was in Depot at Pindi, but I wint circumspectuous, for well I knew 'tis just at the rump-ind av all things that his luck turns on a man. By token I ad seen a dhriver of a batthery goin' by at a trot singin' 'Home, swate home' at the top av his shout, and takin' no heed o his bridle-hand—I had seen that man dhrop under the gun in the middle of a word, and come out by the limber like—like a frog on a pave-stone. No. I wud not hurry, though, God knows, my heart was all in Pindi. Love-o'-Women saw fwhat was in my mind, an' 'Go on, Terence,' h sez, 'I know fwhat's waitin' for you.' 'I will not,' I sez. ''Twill kape a little yet.'

"Ye know the turn of the pass forninst Jumrood and the nine mile road on the flat to Peshawur? All Peshawur was along that road day and night waitin' for frinds—men, women, childer, and bands. Some av the throops was camped round Jumrood, an' some went on to Peshawur to get away down to their cantonmints. We came through in the early mornin', havin' been awake the night through, and we dhruv sheer into the middle av the mess. Mother av Glory, will I ever forget that comin' back? The light was not fair lifted, and the furst we heard was 'For 'tis my delight av a shiny night,' frum a band that thought we was the second four comp'nies av the Lincolnshire. At that we was forced to sind them a yell to say who we was, an' thin up wint 'The wearin' av the Green.' It made me crawl all up my backbone, not havin' taken my brequist. Thin, right smash into our rear, came fwhat was left av the Jock Elliotts—wid four pipers an' not half a kilt among thim, playin' for the dear life, an' swingin' their rumps like buck rabbits, an' a native rig'mint shrieking blue murther. Ye niver heard the like. There was men cryin' like women that did—an' faith I do not blame thim. Fwhat bruk me down was the Lancers' Band—shinin' an' spick like angels, wid the ould dhrum-horse at the head an' the silver kettle-dhrums an' all an' all, waitin' for their men that was behind us. They shtruck up the Cavalry Canter, an', begad, those poor ghosts that had not a sound fut in a throop they answered to ut, the men rockin' in their saddles. We thried to cheer them as they wint by, but ut came out like a big gruntin' cough, so there must have been many that was feelin' like me. Oh, but I'm forgettin'! The Fly-by-Nights was waitin' for their second battalion, an' whin ut came out, there was the Colonel's horse led at the head—saddle-empty. The men fair worshipped him, an' he'd died at Au Musjid on the road down. They waited till the remnint av the battalion was up, and thin—clane against ordhers, for who wanted that chune that day?—they wint back to Peshawur slow-time an' tearin' the bowils out av ivry man that heard, wid 'The Dead March.' Right across our line they wint, an' ye know their uniforms are as black as the Sweeps, crawlin' past like the dead, an' the other bands damnin' them to let be.

"Little they cared. The carpse was wid them, an' they'd ha' taken ut so through a Coronation. Our ordhers was to go into Peshawur, an' we wint hot-fut past the Fly-by-Nights, not singin', to lave that chune behind us. That was how we tuk the road of the other corps.

"'Twas ringin' in my ears still whin I felt in the bones of me that Dinah was comin', an' I heard a shout, an' thin I saw a horse an' a tattoo latherin' down the road, hell to shplit, under women. I knew—I knew! Wan was the Tyrone Colonel's wife—ould Beeker's lady—her gray hair flyin' an' her fat round carkiss rowlin' in the saddle, an' the other was Dinah, that shud ha' been at Pindi. The Colonel's lady she charged at the head av our column like a stone wall, an' she all but knocked Beeker off his horse throwin' her arms round his neck an' blubberin', 'Me bhoy! Me bhoy!' an' Dinah wheeled left an' came down our flank, an' I let a yell that had suffered inside av me for months, and—Dinah came. Will I iver forget that while I live! She'd come on pass from Pindi, an' the Colonel's lady had lint her the tattoo. They'd been huggin' an' cryin' in each other's arms all the long night.

"So she walked along wid her hand in mine, askin' forty questions to wanst, an' beggin' me on the Virgin to make oath that there was not a bullet consaled in me, unbeknownst somewhere, an' thin I remimbered Love-o'-Women. He was watchin' us, an' his face was like the face av a divil that has been cooked too long. I did not wish Dinah to see ut, for whin a woman's runnin' over wid happiness she's like to be touched, for harm afterwards, by the laste little thing in life. So I dhrew the curtain, an' Love-o'-Women lay back and groaned.

"Whin we marched into Peshawur, Dinah wint to barracks to wait for me, an' me feelin' so rich that tide, I wint on to take Love-o'-Women to hospital. It was the last I cud do, an' to save him the dust an' the smother I turned the doolie-men down a road well clear av the rest av the throops, an we wint along, me talkin' through the curtains. Av a sudden I heard him say:—

"'Let me look. For the Mercy av Hiven, let me look!' I had been so tuk up wid gettin' him out av the dust and thinkin' of Dinah that I had not kept my eyes about me. There was a woman ridin' a little behind av us, an', talkin' ut over wid Dinah afterwards, that same woman must ha' rid not far on the Jumrood road. Dinah said that she had been hoverin' like a kite on the left flank av the column.

"I halted the doolie to set the curtains, an' she rode by walkin'-pace, an' Love-o'-Women's eyes wint afther her as if he would fair haul her down from the saddle.

"'Follow there,' was all he sez, but I niver heard a man spake in that voice before or since, an' I knew by those two wan words an' the look in his face that she was Di'monds-an'-Pearls that he'd talked av in his disthresses.

"We followed till she turned into the gate av a little house that stud near the Edwardes's Gate. There was two girls in the verandah, an' they ran in whin they saw us. Faith, at long eye-range ut did not take me a wink to see fwhat kind av house ut was. The throops bein' there an' all, there was three or four such, but afterwards the polis bade them go. At the verandah Love-o'-Women sez, catchin' his breath, 'Stop here,' an' thin, an' thin, wid a grunt that must ha' tore the heart up from his stomach, he swung himself out av the doolie, an' my troth he stud up on his feet wid the sweat pourin' down his face. If Mackie was to walk in here now I'd be less tuk back than I was thin. Where he'd dhrawn his power from, God knows or the divil—but 't was a dead man walkin' in the sun wid the face av a dead man and the breath av a dead man held up by the Power, an' the legs an' the arms of the carpse obeyin' ordhers!

"The woman stud in the verandah. She'd been a beauty too, though her eyes was sunk in her head, an' she looked Love-o'-Women up an' down terrible. 'An',' she sez, kickin' back the tail av her habit,—'An',' she sez, 'fwhat are you doin' here, married man?'

"Love-o'-Women said nothin', but a little froth came to his lips, an' he wiped ut off wid his hand an' looked at her an' the paint on her, an' looked, an' looked, an' looked.

"'An' yet,' she sez, wid a laugh. (Did you hear Mrs. Raines laugh whin Mackie died? Ye did not? Well for you.) 'An' yet,' she sez, 'who but you have betther right,' sez she. 'You taught me the road. You showed me the way,' she sez. 'Ay, look,' she sez, 'for 'tis your work; you that tould me— d'you remimber it?—that a woman who was false to wan man cud be false to two. I have been that,' she sez, 'that an' more, for you always said I was a quick learner, Ellis. Look well,' she sez, 'for it is me that you called your wife in the sight av God long since!' An' she laughed.

"Love-o'-Women stud still in the sun widout answerin'. Thin he groaned an' coughed to wanst, an' I thought 'twas the death-rattle, but he niver tuk his eyes off her face not for a wink. Ye cud ha' put her eyelashes through the flies av an E. P. tent, they were so long.

"'Fwhat do you do here?' she sez, word by word, 'that have taken away my joy in my man this five years gone—that have broken my rest an' killed my body an' damned my soul for the sake av seem' how 'twas done? Did your expayrience afthwards bring you acrost any woman that gave more than I did? Wud I not ha' died for you an' wid you, Ellis? Ye know that, man! If ever your lyin' sowl saw truth in uts life ye know that.'

"An' Love-o'-Women lifted up his head and said, 'I knew,' an' that was all. While she was spakin' the Power hild him up parade-set in the 'sun, an the sweat dhropped undher his helmet. 'Twas more an' more throuble for him to talk, an' his mouth was runnin' twistways.

"Fwhat do you do here?' she sez, an' her voice whit up. 'Twas like bells tollin' before. 'Time was whin you were quick enough wid your words,— you that talked me down to hell. Are ye dumb now?' An' Love-o'-W omen got his tongue, an' sez simple, like a little child, 'May I come in?' he sez.

"The house is open day an' night,' she sez, wid a laugh; an' Love-o'-Women ducked his head an' hild up his hand as tho' he was gyardin'. The Power was on him still—it hild up still, for, by my sowl, as I'll never save ut, he walked up the verandah steps that had been a livin' corpse in hospital for a month!

"'An' now'?' she sez, lookin' at him; an' the red paint stud lone on the white av her face like a bull's-eye on a target.

"He lifted up his eyes, slow an' very slow, an' he looked at her long an' very long, an' he tuk his spache betune his teeth wid a wrench that shuk him.

"'I'm dyin', Aigypt—dyin',' he sez; ay, those were his words, for I remimber the name he called her. He was turnin' the death-colour, but his eyes niver rowled. They were set—set on her. Widout word or warnin' she opened her arms full stretch, an' 'Here!' she sez. (Oh, fwhat a golden mericle av a voice ut was!) 'Die here,' she sez; an' Love-o'-Women dhropped forward, an' she hild him up, for she was a fine big woman.

"I had no time to turn, bekaze that minut I heard the sowl quit him— tore out in the death-rattle—an' she laid him back in a long chair, an' she sez to me, 'Misther soldier,' she sez, 'will ye not go in an' talk to wan av the girls. This sun's too much for him.'

"Well I knew there was no sun he'd iver see, but I cud not spake, so I wint away wid the empty doolie to find the docthor. He'd been breakfastin' an' lunchin' ever since we'd come in, an' he was as full as a tick.

"Faith ye've got dhrunk mighty soon,' he sez, whin I'd tould him, 'to see that man walk. Barrin' a puff or two av life, he was a corpse before we left Jumrood. I've a great mind,' he sez, 'to confine you.'

"'There's a dale av liquor runnin' about, docthor,' I sez, solemn as a hard-boiled egg. 'Maybe 'tis so, but will ye not come an' see the corpse at the house?'

"'Tis dishgraceful,' he sez, 'that I would be expected to go to a place like that. Was she a pretty woman?" he sez, an' at that he set off double quick.

"I cud see that the two was in the verandah were I'd left them, an' I knew by the hang av her head an' the noise av the crows fwhat had happened. 'Twas the first and the last time that I'd ever known woman to use the pistol. They dread the shot as a rule, but Di'monds-an'-Pearls she did not—she did not.

"The docthor touched the long black hair av her head ('twas all loose upon Love-o'-Women's chest), an' that cleared the liquor out av him. He stud considherin' a long time, his hands in his pockets, an' at last he sez to me, 'Here's a double death from naturil causes, most naturil causes; an' in the presint state av affairs the rig'mint will be thankful for wan grave the less to dig. Issiwasti,' he sez, 'Issiwasti, Privit Mulvaney, these two will be buried together in the Civil Cemet'ry at my expinse, an' may the good God,' he sez, 'make it SO much for me whin my time comes. Go to your wife,' he sez; 'go an' be happy. I'll see to this all.'

"I left him still considherin'. They was buried in the Civil Cemet'ry together, wid a Church of England service. There was too many buryin's thin to ask questions, an' the docthor—he ran away wid Major—Major Van Dyce's lady that year—he saw to ut all. Fwhat the right an' the wrong av Love-o'-Women an' Di'monds-an'-Pearls was I niver knew, an' I will niver know; but I've tould ut as I came acrost ut—here an' there in little pieces. So, being fwhat I am, an' knowin' fwhat I know, that's fwhy I say in this shootin'-case here, Mackie that's dead an' in hell is the lucky man. There are times, Sorr, whin 'tis betther for the man to die than to live, an' by consequince forty million times betther for the woman."

"H'up there!" said Ortheris. "It's time to go." The witnesses and guard formed up in the thick white dust of the parched twilight and swung off, marching easy and whistling. Down the road to the green by the church I could hear Ortheris, the black Book-lie still uncleansed on his lips, setting, with a fine sense of the fitness of things, the shrill quick-step that runs—

> *"Oh, do not despise the advice of the wise,*
>
> *Learn wisdom from those that are older,*
>
> *And don't try for things that are out of your reach—*
>
> *An' that's what the Girl told the Soldier*
>
> *Soldier! Soldier!*
>
> *Oh, that's what the Girl told the Soldier!"*

THE BIG DRUNK DRAF'

We're goin' 'ome, we're goin' 'ome—

Our ship is at the shore,

An' you mus' pack your 'aversack,

For we won't come back no more.

Ho, don't you grieve for me,

My lovely Mary Ann,

For I'll marry you yet on a fourp'ny bit,

As a time-expired ma-a-an

Barrack Room Ballad.

AN awful thing has happened! My friend, Private Mulvaney, who went home in the Serapis, time-expired, not very long ago, has come back to India as a civilian! It was all Dinah Shadd's fault. She could not stand the poky little lodgings, and she missed her servant Abdullah more than words could tell. The fact was that the Mulvaneys had been out here too long, and had lost touch of England.

Mulvaney knew a contractor on one of the new Central India lines, and wrote to him for some sort of work. The contractor said that if Mulvaney could pay the passage he would give him command of a gang of coolies for old sake's sake. The pay was eighty-five rupees a month, and Dinah Shadd said that if Terence did not accept she would make his life a "basted purgathory." Therefore the Mulvaneys came out as "civilians," which was a great and terrible fall; though Mulvaney tried to disguise it by saying that he was "Ker'nel on the railway line, an' a consequinshal man."

He wrote me an invitation, on a tool-indent form, to visit him; and I came down to the funny little "construction" bungalow at the side of the line. Dinah Shadd had planted peas about and about, and nature had spread all manner of green stuff round the place. There was no change in Mulvaney except the change of clothing, which was deplorable, but could not be helped. He was standing upon his trolly, haranguing a gangman, and his shoulders were as well drilled and his big, thick chin was as clean-shaven as ever.

"I'm a civilian now," said Mulvaney. "Cud you tell that I was iver a martial man'? Don't answer, Sorr, av you're strainin' betune a complimint an' a lie. There's no houldin' Dinah Shadd now she's got a house av her own. Go inside, an' dhrink tay out av chiny in the drrrrawin'-room, an' thin we'll dhrink like Christians undher the tree here. Scutt, ye naygur-folk! There's a Sahib come to call on me, an' that's more than he'll iver do for you onless you run! Get out, an' go on pilin' up the earth, quick, till sundown."

When we three were comfortably settled under the big sisham in front of the bungalow, and the first rush of questions and answers about Privates Ortheris and Learoyd and old times and places had died away, Mulvaney said, reflectively—"Glory be, there's no p'rade to-morrow, an' no bun-headed Corp'ril-bhoy to give you his lip. An' yit I don't know. 'Tis harrd to be something ye niver were an' niver meant to be, an' all the ould days shut up along wid your papers. Eyah! I'm growin' rusty, an' 'tis the will av God that a man mustn't serve his Quane for time an' all."

He helped himself to a fresh peg, and sighed furiously.

"Let your beard grow, Mulvaney," said I, "and then you won't be troubled with those notions. You'll be a real civilian."

Dinah Shadd had told me in the drawing-room of her desire to coax Mulvaney into letting his beard grow. "'Twas so civilian-like," said poor Dinah, who hated her husband's hankering for his old life.

"Dinah Shadd, you're a dishgrace to an honust, clane-scraped man!" said Mulvaney, without replying to me. "Grow a beard on your own chin, darlint, and lave my razors alone. They're all that stand betune me and dis-ris-pect-ability. Av I didn't shave, I wud be torminted wid an outrajis thurrst; for there's nothin' so dhryin' to the throat as a big billy-goat beard waggin' undher the chin. Ye wudn't have me dhrink always, Dinah Shadd'? By the same token, you're kapin' me crool dhry now. Let me look at that whiskey."

The whiskey was lent and returned, but Dinah Shadd, who had been just as eager as her husband in asking after old friends, rent me with—

"I take shame for you, Sorr, coming down here though the Saints know you're as welkim as the daylight whin you do come—an' upsettin' Terence's head wid your nonsense about—about fwhat's much betther forgotten. He bein' a civilian now, an' you niver was aught else. Can you not let the Arrmy rest? 'Tis not good for Terence."

I took refuge by Mulvaney, for Dinah Shadd has a temper of her own.

"Let be—let be," said Mulvaney. "'Tis only wanst in a way I can talk about the ould days." Then to me—"Ye say Dhrumshticks is well, an' his lady tu'? I niver knew how I liked the gray garron till I was shut av him an' Asia."—"Dhrumshticks" was the nickname of the Colonel commanding Mulvaney's old regiment.—"Will you be seein' him again? You will. Thin tell him"—Mulvaney's eyes began to twinkle—"tell him wid Privit—"

"Mister, Terence," interrupted Dinah Shadd. "Now the Divil an' all his angils an' the Firmament av Hiven fly away wid the 'Mister,' an' the sin av makin' me swear be on your confession, Dinah Shadd! Privit, I tell ye. Wid Privit Mulvaney's best obedience, that but for me the last time-expired wud be still pullin' hair on their way to the sea."

He threw himself back in the chair, chuckled, and was silent.

"Mrs. Mulvaney," I said, "please take up the whiskey, and don't let him have it until he has told the story."

Dinah Shadd dexterously whipped the bottle away, saying at the same time, "'Tis nothing to be proud av," and thus captured by the enemy, Mulvaney spake:—

"'Twas on Chuseday week. I was behaderin' round wid the gangs on the 'bankmint—I've taught the hoppers how to kape step an' stop screechin'—whin a head-gangman comes up to me, wid about two inches av shirt-tail hanging round his neck an' a disthressful light in his oi. 'Sahib,' sez he, 'there's a reg'mint an' a half av soldiers up at the junction, knockin' red cinders out av ivrything an' ivrybody! They thried to hang me in my cloth,' he sez, 'an' there will be murdher an' ruin an' rape in the place before nightfall! They say they're comin' down here to wake us up. What will we do wid our women-folk?'

"'Fetch my throlly!' sez I; 'my heart's sick in my ribs for a wink at anything wid the Quane's uniform on ut. Fetch my throlly, an' six av the jildiest men, and run me up in shtyle.'"

"He tuk his best coat," said Dinah Shadd, reproachfully.

"'Twas to do honour to the Widdy. I cud ha' done no less, Dinah Shadd. You and your digresshins interfere wid the coorse av the narrative. Have you iver considhered fwhat I wud look like wid me head shaved as well as me chin? You bear that in your mind, Dinah darlin'.

"I was throllied up six miles, all to get a shquint at that draf'. I knew 'twas a spring draf' goin' home, for there's no rig'mint hereabouts, more's the pity."

"Praise the Virgin!" murmured Dinah Shadd. But Mulvaney did not hear.

"Whin I was about three-quarters av a mile off the rest-camp, powtherin' along fit to burrst, I heard the noise av the men, an', on my sowl, Sorr, I cud catch the voice av Peg Barney bellowin' like a bison wid the belly-ache. You remimber Peg Barney that was in D Comp'ny—a red, hairy scraun, wid a scar on his jaw? Peg Barney that cleared out the Blue Lights' Jubilee meetin' wid the cook-room mop last year?

"Thin I knew ut was a draf' av the Ould Rig'mint, an' I was conshumed wid sorrow for the bhoy that was in charge. We was harrd scrapin's at any time. Did I iver tell you how Horker Kelley wint into clink nakid as Phoebus Apollonius, wid the shirts av the Corp'ril an' file undher his arrum? An' he was a moild man! But I'm digresshin'. 'Tis a shame both to the rig'mints and the Arrmy sendin' down little orf'cer bhoys wid a draf' av strong men mad wid liquor an' the chanst av gettin' shut av India, an' niver a punishment that's fit to be given right down an' away from cantonmints to the dock! 'Tis this nonsinse. Whin I am servin' my time, I'm undher the Articles av War, an' can be whipped on the peg for thim. But whin I've served my time, I'm a Reserve man, an' the Articles av War haven't any hould on me. An orf'cer can't do anythin' to a time-expired savin' confinin' him to barricks. 'Tis a wise rig'lation, bekaze a time-expired does not have any barricks; bein' on the move all the time. 'Tis a Solomon av a rig'lation, is that. I wud like to be inthroduced to the man that made ut. 'Tis easier to get colts from a Kibbereen horse-fair into Galway than to take a bad draf' over ten miles av counthry. Consiquintly that rig'lation—for fear that the men wud be hurt by the little orf'cer bhoy. No matther. The nearer my throlly came to the rest-camp, the woilder was the shine, an' the louder was the voice of Peg Barney. "Tis good I am here,' thinks I to mysilf, 'for Peg alone is employmint for two or three.' He bein', I well knew, as copped as a dhrover.

"Faith, that rest-camp was a sight! The tent-ropes was all skew-nosed, an' the pegs looked as dhrunk as the men—fifty av thim—the scourin's, an' rinsin's, an' Divil's lavin's av the Ould Rig'mint. I tell you, Sorr, they were dhrunker than any men you've ever seen in your mortial life. How does a draf' get dhrunk? How does a frog get fat? They suk ut in through their shkins.

"There was Peg Barney sittin' on the groun' in his shirt—wan shoe off an' wan shoe on—whackin' a tent-peg over the head wid his boot, an' singin' fit to wake the dead. 'Twas no clane song that he sung, though. 'Twas the Divil's Mass."

"What's that?" I asked.

"Whin a bad egg is shut av the Army, he sings the Divil's Mass for a good riddance; an' that manes swearin' at ivrything from the Commandherin-Chief down to the Room-Corp'ril, such as you niver in your days heard. Some men can swear so as to make green turf crack! Have you iver heard the Curse in an Orange Lodge? The Divil's Mass is ten times worse, an' Peg Barney was singin' ut, whackin' the tent-peg on the head wid his boot for each man that he cursed. A powerful big voice had Peg Barney, an' a hard swearer he was whin sober. I stood forninst him, an' 'twas not me oi alone that cud tell Peg was dhrunk as a coot.

"Good mornin', Peg,' I sez, whin he dhrew breath afther dursin' the Adj'tint-Gen'ral; 'I've put on my best coat to see you, Peg Barney,' sez I.

"Thin take Ut off again,' sez Peg Barney, latherin' away wid the boot; 'take ut off an' dance, ye lousy civilian!'

"Wid that he begins cursin' ould Dhrumshticks, being so full he dane disrernimbers the Brigade-Major an' the Judge-Advokit-Gen'ral.

"Do you not know me, Peg?' sez I, though me blood was hot in me wid being called a civilian."

"An' him a decent married man!" wailed Dinah Shadd.

"I do not," sez Peg, "but dhrunk or sober I'll tear the hide off your back wid a shovel whin I've stopped singin."

"'Say you so, Peg Barney?' sez I. "Tis clear as mud you've forgotten me. I'll assist your autobiography.' Wid that I stretched Peg Barney, boot an' all, an' wint into the camp. An awful sight ut was!

"'Where's the orf'cer in charge av the detachment?' sez I to Scrub Greene—the manest little worm that ever walked.

"'There's no orf'cer, ye ould cook,' sez Scrub; 'we're a bloomin' Republic.'

"'Are you that?' sez I; 'thin I'm O'Connell the Dictator, an' by this you will larn to kape a civil tongue in your rag-box.'

"Wid that I stretched Scrub Greene an' wint to the orf'cer's tent. 'Twas a new little bhoy—not wan I'd iver seen before. He was sittin' in his tent, purtendin' not to 'ave ear av the racket.

"I saluted—but for the life av me I mint to shake hands whin I went in. 'Twas the sword hangin' on the tent-pole changed my will.

"'Can't I help, Sorr?' sez I; "tis a strong man's job they've given you, an' you'll be wantin' help by sundown.' He was a bhoy wid bowils, that child, an' a rale gintleman.

"'Sit down,' sez he.

"'Not before my orf'cer,' sez I; an' I tould him fwhat my service was.

"'I've heard av you,' sez he. 'You tuk the town av Lungtungpen nakid.'

"'Faith,' thinks I, 'that's Honour an' Glory'; for 'twas Lift'nint Brazenose did that job. 'I'm wid ye, Sorr,' sez I, 'if I'm av use. They shud niver ha' sent you down wid the draf'. Savin' your presince, Sorr,' I sez, "tis only Lift'nint Hackerston in the Ould Rig'mint can manage a Home draf'.'

"'I've niver had charge of men like this before,' sez he, playin' wid the pens on the table; 'an' I see by the Rig'lations—'

"'Shut your oi to the Rig'lations, Sorr,' I sez, 'till the throoper's into blue wather. By the Rig'lations you've got to tuck thim up for the night, or they'll be runnin' foul av my coolies an' makin' a shiverarium half through the counthry. Can you trust your noncoms, Sorr?'

"'Yes,' sez he.

"'Good,' sez I; 'there'll be throuble before the night. Are you marchin', Sorr?'

"'To the next station,' sez he.

"'Betther still,' sez I; 'there'll be big throuble.'

"'Can't be too hard on a Home draf,' sez he; 'the great thing is to get thim in-ship.'

"'Faith, you've larnt the half av your lesson, Sorr,' sez I, 'but av you shtick to the Rig'lations you'll niver get thim inship at all, at all. Or there won't be a rag av kit betune thim whin you do.'

"'Twas a dear little orf'cer bhoy, an' by way av kapin' his heart up, I tould him fwhat I saw wanst in a draf in Egypt."

"What was that, Mulvaney?" said I.

"Sivin an' fifty men sittin' on the bank av a canal, laughin' at a poor little squidgereen av an orf'cer that they'd made wade into the slush an' pitch things out av the boats for their Lord High Mightinesses. That made me orf'cer bhoy woild wid indignation.

"'Soft an' aisy, Sorr,' sez I; 'you've niver had your draf' in hannd since you left cantonmints Wait till the night, an' your work will be ready to you. Wid your permission, Sorr, I will investigate the camp, an' talk to me ould frinds. 'Tis no manner av use thryin' to shtop the divilmint now.'

"Wid that I wint out into the camp an' inthrojuced mysilf to ivry man sober enough to remimber me. I was some wan in the ould days, an' the bhoys was glad to see me—all excipt Peg Barney wid a eye like a tomata five days in the bazar, an' a nose to match. They come round me an' shuk me, an' I tould thim I was in privit employ wid an income av me own, an' a drrrawin'-room fit to bate the Quane's; an' wid me lies an' me shtories an' nonsinse gin'rally, I kept 'em quiet in wan way an' another, knockin' roun' the camp. 'Twas bad even thin whin I was the Angil av Peace.

"I talked to me ould non-coms—they was sober—an' betune me an' thim we wore the draf' over into their tents at the proper time. The little orf'cer bhoy he conies round, dacint an' civil-spoken as might be.

"'Rough quarthers, men,' sez he, 'but you can't look to be as comfortable as in barricks. We must make the best av things. I've shut my eyes to a dale av dog's thricks to-day, an' now there must be no more av ut.'

"No more we will. Come an' have a dhrink, me son,' sez Peg Barney, staggerin' where he stud. Me little orf'cer bhoy kep' his timper.

"'You're a sulky swine, you are,' sez Peg Barney, an' at that the men in the tent began to laugh.

"I tould you me orf'cer bhoy had bowils. He cut Peg Barney as near as might be on the oi that I'd squshed whin we first met. Peg wint spinnin' acrost the tent.

"Peg him out, Sorr,' sez I, in a whishper.

"Peg him out!' sez me orf'cer bhoy, up loud, just as if 'twas battalion p'rade an' he pickin' his wurrds from the Sargint.

"The non-coms tuk Peg Barney—a howlin' handful he was—an' in three minut's he was pegged out—chin down, tight-dhrawn—on his stummick, a tent-peg to each arm an' leg, swearin' fit to turn a naygur white.

"I tuk a peg an'' jammed ut into his ugly jaw—'Bite on that, Peg Barney,' I sez; 'the night is settin' frosty, an' you'll be wantin' divarsion before the mornin'. But for the Rig'lations you'd be bitin' on a bullet now at the thriangles, Peg Barney,' sez I.

"All the draf' was out av their tents watchin' Barney bein' pegged.

"'Tis agin the Rig'lations! He strook him!' screeches out Scrub Greene, who was always a lawyer; an' some of the men tuk up the shoutin'.

"'Peg out that man!' sez me orf'cer bhoy, niver losin' his timper; an' the non-coms wint in and pegged out Scrub Greene by the side av Peg Barney.

"I cud see that the draf' was comin' roun'. The men stud not knowin' fwhat to do.

"'Get to your tents!' sez me orf'cer bhoy. 'Sargint, put a sinthry over these two men.'

"The men wint back into the tents like jackals, an' the rest av the night there was no noise at all excipt the stip av the sinthry over the two, an' Scrub Greene blubberin' like a child. 'Twas a chilly night, an' faith, ut sobered Peg Barney.

"Just before Revelly, me orf'cer bhoy comes out an' sez: 'Loose those men an' send thim to their tents!' Scrub Greene wint away widout a word, but Peg Barney, stiff wid the cowld, stud like a sheep, thryin' to make his orf'cer undherstand he was sorry for playin' the goat.

"There was no tucker in the draf' whin ut fell in for the march, an' divil a wurrd about 'illegality' cud I hear.

"I wint to the ould Colour-Sargint and I sez:—'Let me die in glory,' sez I. 'I've seen a man this day!'

"'A man he is,' sez ould Hother; 'the draf's as sick as a herrin'. They'll all go down to the sea like lambs. That bhoy has the bowils av a cantonmint av Gin'rals.'

"'Amin,' sez I, 'an' good luck go wid him, wheriver he be, by land or by sea. Let me know how the draf' gets clear.'

"An' do you know how they did? That bhoy, so I was tould by letter from Bombay, bully-damned 'em down to the dock, till they cudn't call their sowls their own. From the time they left me oi till they was 'tween decks, not wan av thim was more than dacintly dhrunk. An' by the Holy Articles av War, whin they wint aboord they cheered him till they cudn't spake, an' that, mark you, has not come about wid a draf' in the mlm'ry av livin' man! You look to that little orf'cer bhoy. He has bowils. 'Tis not ivry child that wud chuck the Rig'lations to Flanders an' stretch Peg Barney on a wink from a brokin an' dilapidated ould carkiss like mysilf. I'd be proud to serve—"

"Terence, you're a civilian," said Dinah Shadd warningly.

"So I am—so I am. Is ut likely I wud forget ut? But he was a gran' bhoy all the same, an' I'm only a mudtipper wid a hod on me shoulthers. The whiskey's in the heel av your hand, Sorr. Wid your good lave we'll dhrink to the Ould Rig'mint—three fingers—standin' up!" And we drank.

THE MUTINEY OF THE MAVERICKS

Sec. 7 (1)—Causing or Conspiring with other persons to cause a mutiny or sedition in forces belonging to Her Majesty's Regular forces, Reserve forces, Auxiliary forces, or Navy.

When three obscure gentlemen in San Francisco argued on insufficient premises they condemned a fellow-creature to a most unpleasant death in a far country which had nothing whatever to do with the United States. They foregathered at the top of a tenement-house in Tehama Street, an unsavoury quarter of the city, and, there calling for certain drinks, they conspired because they were conspirators by trade, officially known as the Third Three of the I. A. A.—an institution for the propagation of pure light, not to be confounded with any others, though it is affiliated to many. The Second Three live in Montreal, and work among the poor there; the First Three have their home in New York, not far from Castle Garden, and write regularly once a week to a small house near one of the big hotels at Boulogne. What happens after that, a particular section of Scotland Yard knows too well and laughs at. A conspirator detests ridicule. More men have been stabbed with Lucrezia Borgia daggers and dropped into the Thames for laughing at Head Centres and Triangles than for betraying secrets; for this is human nature.

The Third Three conspired over whiskey cocktails and a clean sheet of note-paper against the British Empire and all that lay therein. This work is very like what men without discernment call politics before a general election. You pick out and discuss, in the company of congenial friends, all the weak points in your opponents' organisation, and unconsciously dwell upon and exaggerate all their mishaps, till it seems to you a miracle that the hated party holds together for an hour.

"Our principle is not so much active demonstration—that we leave to others—as passive embarrassment, to weaken and unnerve," said the first man. "Wherever an organisation is crippled, wherever confusion is thrown into any branch of any department, we gain a step for those who take on the work; we are but the forerunners." He was a German enthusiast, and editor of a newspaper, from whose leading articles he quoted frequently.

"That cursed Empire makes so many blunders of her own that unless we doubled the year's average I guess it wouldn't strike her anything special had occurred," said the second man. "Are you prepared to say that all our resources are equal to blowing off the muzzle of a hundred-ton gun or spiking a ten-thousand-ton ship on a plain rock in clear daylight? They can beat us at our own game. Better join hands with the practical branches; we're in funds now. Try a direct scare in a crowded street. They value their greasy hides." He was the drag upon the wheel, and an Americanised Irishman of the second generation, despising his own race and hating the other. He had learned caution.

The third man drank his cocktail and spoke no word. He was the strategist, but unfortunately his knowledge of life was limited. He picked a letter from his breast-pocket and threw it across the table. That epistle to the heathen contained some very concise directions from the First Three in New York. It said—

"The boom in black iron has already affected the eastern markets, where our agents have been forcing down the English-held stock among the smaller buyers who watch the turn of shares. Any immediate operations, such as western bears, would increase their willingness to unload. This, however, cannot be expected till they see clearly that foreign iron-masters are willing to co-operate. Mulcahy should be dispatched to feel the pulse of the market, and act accordingly. Mavericks are at present the best for our purpose.—P. D. Q."

As a message referring to an iron crisis in Pennsylvania, it was interesting, if not lucid. As a new departure in organized attack on an outlying English dependency, it was more than interesting.

The second man read it through and murmured—"Already? Surely they are in too great a hurry. All that Dhulip Singh could do in India he has done, down to the distribution of his photographs among the peasantry. Ho! Ho! The Paris firm arranged that, and he has no substantial money backing from the Other Power. Even our agents in India know he hasn't. What is the use of our organisation wasting men on work that is already done? Of course the Irish regiments in India are half mutinous as they stand."

This shows how near a lie may come to the truth. An Irish regiment, for just so long as it stands still, is generally a hard handful to control, being reckless and rough. When, however, it is moved in the direction of musketry-firing, it becomes strangely and unpatriotically content with its lot. It has even been heard to cheer the Queen with enthusiasm on these occasions.

But the notion of tampering with the army was, from the point of view of Tehama Street, an altogether sound one. There is no shadow of stability in the policy of an English Government, and the most sacred oaths of England would, even if engrossed on vellum, find very few buyers among colonies and dependencies that have suffered from vain beliefs. But there remains to England always her army. That cannot change except in the matter of uniform and equipment. The officers may write to the papers demanding the heads of the Horse Guards in default of cleaner redress for grievances; the men may break loose across a country town and seriously startle the publicans; but neither officers nor men have it in their composition to mutiny after the continental manner. The English people, when they trouble to think about the army at all, are, and with justice, absolutely assured that it is absolutely trustworthy. Imagine for a moment their emotions on realising that such and such a regiment was in open revolt from causes directly due to England's management of Ireland. They would probably send the regiment to the polls forthwith and examine their own consciences as to their duty to Erin; but they would never be easy any more. And it was this vague, unhappy mistrust that the I. A. A. were labouring to produce.

"Sheer waste of breath," said the second man after a pause in the council. "I don't see the use of tampering with their fool-army, but it has been tried before and we must try it again. It looks well in the reports. If we send one man from here you may bet your life that other men are going too. Order up Mulcahy."

They ordered him up—a slim, slight, dark-haired young man, devoured with that blind rancorous hatred of England that only reaches its full growth across the Atlantic. He had sucked it from his mother's breast in the little cabin at the back of the northern avenues of New York; he had been taught his rights and his wrongs, in German and Irish, on the canal fronts of Chicago; and San Francisco held men who told him strange and awful things of the great blind power over the seas. Once, when business took him across the Atlantic, he had served in an English regiment, and being insubordinate had suffered extremely. He drew all his ideas of England that were not bred by the cheaper patriotic prints from one iron-fisted colonel and an unbending adjutant. He would go to the mines if need be to teach his gospel. And he went, as his instructions advised, p. d. q.—which means "with speed"—to introduce embarrassment into an Irish regiment, "already half-mutinous, quartered among Sikh peasantry, all wearing miniatures of His Highness Dhulip Singh, Maharaja of the Punjab, next their hearts, and all eagerly expecting his arrival." Other information equally valuable was given him by his masters. He was to be cautious, but never to grudge expense in winning the hearts of the men in the regiment. His mother in New York would supply funds, and he was to write to her once a month. Life is pleasant for a man who has a mother in New York to send him two hundred pounds a year over and above his regimental pay.

In process of time, thanks to his intimate knowledge of drill and musketry exercise, the excellent Mulcahy, wearing the corporal's stripe, went out in a troopship and joined Her Majesty's Royal Loyal Musketeers, commonly known as the "Mavericks," because they were masterless and unbranded cattle—sons of small farmers in County Clare, shoeless vagabonds of Kerry, herders of Ballyvegan, much wanted "moonlighters" from the bare rainy headlands of the south coast, officered by O'Mores, Bradys, Hills, Kilreas, and the like. Never to outward seeming was there more promising material to work on. The First Three had chosen their regiment well. It feared nothing that moved or talked save the colonel and the regimental Roman Catholic chaplain, the fat Father Dennis, who held the keys of heaven and hell, and blared like an angry bull when he desired to be convincing. Him also it loved because on occasions of stress he was used to tuck up his cassock and charge with the rest into the merriest of the fray, where he always found, good man, that the saints sent him a revolver when there was a fallen private to be protected, or—but this came as an afterthought his own gray head to be guarded.

Cautiously as he had been instructed, tenderly and with much beer, Mulcahy opened his projects to such as he deemed fittest to listen. And these were, one and all, of that quaint, crooked, sweet, profoundly irresponsible and profoundly lovable race that fight like fiends, argue like children, reason like women, obey like men, and jest like their own goblins of the rath through rebellion, loyalty, want, woe, or war. The underground work of a conspiracy is always dull and very much the same the world over. At the end of six months—the seed always falling on good ground— Mulcahy spoke almost explicitly, hinting darkly in the approved fashion at dread powers behind him, and advising nothing more nor less than mutiny. Were they not dogs, evilly treated? had they not all their own and their national revenges to satisfy? Who in these days would do aught to nine hundred men in rebellion? Who, again, could stay them if they broke for the sea, licking up on their way other regiments only too anxious to join? And afterwards... here followed windy promises of gold and preferment, office and honour, ever dear to a certain type of Irishman.

As he finished his speech, in the dusk of a twilight, to his chosen associates, there was a sound of a rapidly unslung belt behind him. The arm of one Dan Grady flew out in the gloom and arrested something. Then said Dan—

"Mulcahy, you're a great man, an' you do credit to whoever sent you. Walk about a bit while we think of it." Mulcahy departed elate. He knew his words would sink deep.

"Why the triple-dashed asterisks did ye not let me belt him'?" grunted a voice.

"Because I'm not a fat-headed fool. Boys, 'tis what he's been driving at these six months—our superior corp'ril with his education and his copies of the Irish papers and his everlasting beer. He's been sent for the purpose, and that's where the money comes from. Can ye not see? That man's a gold-mine, which Horse Egan here would have destroyed with a belt-buckle. It would be throwing away the gifts of Providence not to fall in with his little plans. Of coorse we'll mut'ny till all's dry. Shoot the colonel on the parade-ground, massacree the company officers, ransack the arsenal, and then—Boys, did he tell you what next? He told me the other night when he was beginning to talk wild. Then we're to join with the niggers, and look for help from Dhulip Singh and the Russians!"

"And spoil the best campaign that ever was this side of Hell! Danny, I'd have lost the beer to ha' given him the belting he requires."

"Oh, let him go this awhile, man! He's got no—no constructiveness, but that's the egg-meat of his plan, and you must understand that I'm in with it, an' so are you. We'll want oceans of beer to convince us—firmaments full. We'll give him talk for his money, and one by one all the boys'll come in and he'll have a nest of nine hundred mutineers to squat in an' give drink to."

"What makes me killing-mad is his wanting us to do what the niggers did thirty years gone. That an' his pig's cheek in saying that other regiments would come along," said a Kerry man.

"That's not so bad as hintin' we should loose off on the colonel."

"Colonel be sugared! I'd as soon as not put a shot through his helmet to see him jump and clutch his old horse's head. But Mulcahy talks o' shootin' our comp'ny orf'cers accidental."

"He said that, did he?" said Horse Egan.

"Somethin' like that, anyways. Can't ye fancy ould Barber Brady wid a bullet in his lungs, coughin' like a sick monkey, an' sayin', 'Bhoys, I do not mind your gettin' dhrunk, but you must hould your liquor like men. The man that shot me is dhrunk. I'll suspend investigations for six hours, while I get this bullet cut out, and then—'"

"'An' then,' continued Horse Egan, for the peppery Major's peculiarities of speech and manner were as well known as his tanned face; "'an' then, ye dissolute, half-baked, putty-faced scum o' Connemara, if I find a man so much as lookin' confused, begad, I'll coort-martial the whole company. A man that can't get over his liquor in six hours is not fit to belong to the Mavericks!'"

A shout of laughter bore witness to the truth of the sketch.

"It's pretty to think of," said the Kerry man slowly. "Mulcahy would have us do all the devilmint, and get clear himself, someways. He wudn't be takin' all this fool's throuble in shpoilin' the reputation of the regimint—"

"Reputation of your grandmother's pig!" said Dan.

"Well, an' he had a good reputation tu; so it's all right. Mulcahy must see his way to clear out behind him, or he'd not ha' come so far, talkin' powers of darkness."

"Did you hear anything of a regimental coortmartial among the Black Boneens, these days? Half a company of 'em took one of the new draft an' hanged him by his arms with a tent-rope from a third-story verandah. They gave no reason for so doin', but he was half dead. I'm thinking that the Boneens are short-sighted. It was a friend of Mulcahy's, or a man in the same trade. They'd a deal better ha' taken his beer," returned Dan reflectively.

"Better still ha' handed him up to the Colonel," said Horse Egan, "onless—but sure the news wud be all over the counthry an' give the reg'ment a bad name."

"An' there'd be no reward for that man—he but went about talkin'," said the Kerry man artlessly.

"You speak by your breed," said Dan, with a laugh. "There was never a Kerry man yet that wudn't sell his brother for a pipe o' tobacco an' a pat on the back from a p'liceman."

"Praise God I'm not a bloomin' Orangeman," was the answer.

"No, nor never will be," said Dan. "They breed men in Ulster. Would you like to thry the taste of one?"

The Kerry man looked and longed, but forbore. The odds of battle were too great. "Then you'll not even give Mulcahy a—a strike for his money," said the voice of Horse Egan, who regarded what he called "trouble" of any kind as the pinnacle of felicity.

Dan answered not at all, but crept on tip-toe, with long strides, to the mess-room, the men following. The room was empty. In a corner, cased like the King of Dahomey's state umbrella, stood the regimental Colours. Dan lifted them tenderly and unrolled in the light of the candles the record of the Mavericks—tattered, worn, and hacked. The white satin was darkened everywhere with big brown stains, the gold threads on the crowned harp were frayed and discoloured, and the Red Bull, the totem of the Mavericks, was coffee-hued. The stiff, embroidered folds, whose price is human life, rustled down slowly. The Mavericks keep their colours long and guard them very sacredly.

"Vittoria, Salamanca, Toulouse, Waterloo, Moodkee, Ferozshah, an' Sobraon—that was fought close next door here, against the very beggars he wants us to join. Inkerman, The Alma, Sebastopol! 'What are those little businesses compared to the campaigns of General Mulcahy? The Mut'ny, think o' that; the Mut'ny an' some dirty little matters in Afghanistan; an' for that an' these an' those"—Dan pointed to the names of glorious battles— "that Yankee man with the partin' in his hair comes an' says as easy as 'have a drink'... Holy Moses, there's the captain!"

But it was the mess-sergeant who came in just as the men clattered out, and found the colours uncased.

From that day dated the mutiny of the Mavericks, to the joy of Mulcahy and the pride of his mother in New York—the good lady who sent the money for the beer. Never, so far as words went, was such a mutiny. The conspirators, led by Dan Grady and Horse Egan, poured in daily. They were sound men, men to be trusted, and they all wanted blood; but first they must have beer. They cursed the Queen, they mourned over Ireland, they suggested hideous plunder of the Indian country-side, and then, alas— some of the younger men would go forth and wallow on the ground in spasms of wicked laughter The genius of the Irish for conspiracies is remarkable. None the less they would swear no oaths but those of their own making, which were rare and curious, and they were always at pains to impress Mulcahy with the risks they ran. Naturally the flood of beer wrought demoralisation. But Mulcahy confused the causes of things, and when a very muzzy Maverick smote a sergeant on the nose or called his commanding officer a bald-headed old lard-bladder and even worse names, he fancied that rebellion and not liquor was at the bottom of the outbreak. Other gentlemen who have concerned themselves in larger conspiracies have made the same error.

The hot season, in which they protested no man could rebel, came to an end, and Mulcahy suggested a visible return for his teachings. As to the actual upshot of the mutiny he cared nothing. It would be enough if the English, infatuatedly trusting to the integrity of their army, should be startled with news of an Irish regiment revolting from political considerations. His persistent demands would have ended, at Dan's instigation, in a regimental belting which in all probability would have killed him and cut off the supply of beer, had not he been sent on special duty some fifty miles away from the Cantonment to cool his heels in a mud fort and dismount obsolete artillery. Then the colonel of the Mavericks, reading his newspaper diligently, and scenting Frontier trouble from afar, posted to the army headquarters and pled with the Commander-in-chief for certain privileges, to be granted under certain contingencies; which contingencies came about only a week later, when the annual little war on the border developed itself and the colonel returned to carry the good news to the Mavericks. He held the promise of the Chief for active service, and the men must get ready.

On the evening of the same day, Mulcahy, an unconsidered corporal— yet great in conspiracy—returned to cantonments, and heard sounds of strife and howlings from afar off. The mutiny had broken out and the barracks of the Mavericks were one white-washed pandemonium. A private tearing through the barrack-square, gasped in his ear, "Service! Active service. It's a burnin' shame." Oh joy, the Mavericks had risen on the eve of battle! They would not—noble and loyal sons of Ireland—serve the Queen longer. The news would flash through the country-side and over to England, and he—Mulcahy—the trusted of the Third Three, had brought about the crash. The private stood in the middle of the square and cursed colonel, regiment, officers, and doctor, particularly the doctor, by his gods. An orderly of the native cavalry regiment clattered through the mob of soldiers. He was half lifted, half dragged from his horse, beaten on the back with mighty hand-claps till his eyes watered, and called all manner of endearing names. Yes, the Mavericks had fraternized with the native troops. Who then was the agent among the latter that had blindly wrought with Mulcahy so well?

An officer slunk, almost ran, from the mess to a barrack. He was mobbed by the infuriated soldiery, who closed round but did not kill him, for he fought his way to shelter, flying for the life. Mulcahy could have wept with pure joy and thankfulness. The very prisoners in the guard-room were shaking the bars of their cells and howling like wild beasts, and from every barrack poured the booming as of a big war-drum.

Mulcahy hastened to his own barrack. He could hardly hear himself speak. Eighty men were pounding with fist and heel the tables and trestles—eighty men, flushed with mutiny, stripped to their shirt sleeves, their knapsacks half-packed for the march to the sea, made the two-inch boards thunder again as they chanted, to a tune that Mulcahy knew well, the Sacred War Song of the Mavericks—

> *Listen in the north, my boys, there's trouble on the wind;*
>
> *Tramp o' Cossack hooves in front, gray great-coats behind,*
>
> *Trouble on the Frontier of a most amazin' kind,*
>
> *Trouble on the waters o' the Oxus!*

Then, as the table broke under the furious accompaniment—

Hurrah! hurrah! it's north by west we go;

Hurrah! hurrah! the chance we wanted so;

Let 'em hear the chorus from Umballa to Moscow,

As we go marchin' to the Kremling.

"Mother of all the saints in bliss and all the devils in cinders, where's my fine new sock widout the heel?" howled Horse Egan, ransacking everybody's valise but his own. He was engaged in making up deficiencies of kit preparatory to a campaign, and in that work he steals best who steals last. "Ah, Mulcahy, you're in good time," he shouted, "We've got the route, and we're off on Thursday for a pic-nic wid the Lancers next door."

An ambulance orderly appeared with a huge basket full of lint rolls, provided by the forethought of the Queen for such as might need them later on. Horse Egan unrolled his bandage, and flicked it under Mulcahy's nose, chanting—

"Sheepskin an' bees' wax, thunder, pitch, and plaster,

The more you try to pull it off, the more it sticks the faster.

As I was goin' to New Orleans—

"You know the rest of it, my Irish American-Jew boy. By gad, ye have to fight for the Queen in the inside av a fortnight, my darlin.'"

A roar of laughter interrupted. Mulcahy looked vacantly down the room. Bid a boy defy his father when the pantomime-cab is at the door, or a girl develop a will of her own when her mother is putting the last touches to the first ball-dress, but do not ask an Irish regiment to embark upon mutiny on the eve of a campaign, when it has fraternised with the native regiment that accompanies it, and driven its officers into retirement with ten thousand clamorous questions, and the prisoners dance for joy, and the sick men stand in the open calling down all known diseases on the head of the doctor, who has certified that they are "medically unfit for active service." At even the Mavericks might have been mistaken for mutineers by one so unversed in their natures as Mulcahy. At dawn a girls' school might have learned deportment from them. They knew that their colonel's hand had closed, and that he who broke that iron discipline would not go to the front: nothing in the world will persuade one of our soldiers, when he is ordered to the north on the smallest of affairs, that he is not immediately going gloriously to slay Cossacks and cook his kettles in the palace of the Czar. A few of the younger men mourned for Mulcahy's beer, because the campaign was to be conducted on strict temperance principles, but as Dan and Horse Egan said sternly, "We've got the beer-man with us. He shall drink now on his own hook."

Mulcahy had not taken into account the possibility of being sent on active service. He had made up his mind that he would not go under any circumstances, but fortune was against him.

"Sick-you?" said the doctor, who had served an unholy apprenticeship to his trade in Tralee poorhouses. "You're only home-sick, and what you call varicose veins come from over-eating. A little gentle exercise will cure that." And later, "Mulcahy, my man, everybody is allowed to apply for a sick-certificate once. If he tries it twice we call him by an ugly name. Go back to your duty, and let's hear no more of your diseases."

I am ashamed to say that Horse Egan enjoyed the study of Mulcahy's soul in those days, and Dan took an equal interest. Together they would communicate to their corporal all the dark lore of death which is the portion of those who have seen men die. Egan had the larger experience, but Dan the finer imagination. Mulcahy shivered when the former spoke of the knife as an intimate acquaintance, or the latter dwelt with loving particularity on the fate of those who, wounded and helpless, had been overlooked by the ambulances, and had fallen into the hands of the Afghan women-folk.

Mulcahy knew that the mutiny, for the present at least, was dead; knew, too, that a change had come over Dan's usually respectful attitude towards him, and Horse Egan's laughter and frequent allusions to abortive conspiracies emphasised all that the conspirator had guessed. The horrible fascination of the death-stories, however, made him seek the men's society. He learned much more than he had bargained for; and in this manner. It was on the last night before the regiment entrained to the front. The barracks were stripped of everything movable, and the men were too excited to sleep. The bare walls gave out a heavy hospital smell of chloride of lime.

"And what," said Mulcahy in an awe-stricken whisper, after some conversation on the eternal subject, "are you going to do to me, Dan?" This might have been the language of an able conspirator conciliating a weak spirit.

"You'll see," said Dan grimly, turning over in his cot, "or I rather shud say you'll not see."

This was hardly the language of a weak spirit. Mulcahy shook under the bed-clothes.

"Be easy with him," put in Egan from the next cot. "He has got his chanst o' goin' clean. Listen, Mulcahy, all we want is for the good sake of the regiment that you take your death standing up, as a man shud. There's be heaps an' heaps of enemy—plenshus heaps. Go there an' do all you can and die decent. You'll die with a good name there. 'Tis not a hard thing considerin'."

Again Mulcahy shivered.

"An' how could a man wish to die better than fightin'?" added Dan consolingly.

"And if I won't?" said the corporal in a dry whisper.

"There'll be a dale of smoke," returned Dan, sitting up and ticking off the situation on his fingers, "sure to be, an' the noise of the firin'll be tremenjus, an' we'll be running about up and down, the regiment will. But we, Horse and I—we'll stay by you, Mulcahy, and never let you go. Maybe there'll be an accident."

"It's playing it low on me. Let me go. For pity's sake, let me go. I never did you harm, and—and I stood you as much beer as I could. Oh, don't be hard on me, Dan! You are—you were in it too. You won't kill me up there, will you?"

"I'm not thinkin' of the treason; though you shud be glad any honest boys drank with you. It's for the regiment. We can't have the shame o' you bringin' shame on us. You went to the doctor quiet as a sick cat to get and stay behind an' live with the women at the depot—you that wanted us to run to the sea in wolf-packs like the rebels none of your black blood dared to be! But we knew about your goin' to the doctor, for he told in mess, and it's all over the regiment. Bein', as we are, your best friends, we didn't allow any one to molest you yet. We will see to you ourselves. Fight which you will—us or the enemy you'll never lie in that cot again, and there's more glory and maybe less kicks from fightin' the enemy. That's fair speakin'."

"And he told us by word of mouth to go and join with the niggers— you've forgotten that, Dan," said Horse Egan, to justify sentence.

"What's the use of plaguin' the man? One shot pays for all. Sleep ye sound, Mulcahy. But you onderstand, do ye not?"

Mulcahy for some weeks understood very little of anything at all save that ever at his elbow, in camp or at parade, stood two big men with soft voices adjuring him to commit hari-kari lest a worse thing should happen— to die for the honour of the regiment in decency among the nearest knives. But Mulcahy dreaded death. He remembered certain things that priests had said in his infancy, and his mother—not the one at New York—starting from her sleep with shrieks to pray for a husband's soul in torment. It is well to be of a cultured intelligence, but in time of trouble the weak human mind returns to the creed it sucked in at the breast, and if that creed be not a pretty one trouble follows. Also, the death he would have to face would be physically painful. Most conspirators have large imaginations. Mulcahy could see himself, as he lay on the earth in the night, dying by various causes. They were all horrible; the mother in New York was very far away, and the Regiment, the engine that, once you fall in its grip, moves you forward whether you will or won't, was daily coming closer to the enemy!

They were brought to the field of Marzun Katai, and with the Black Boneens to aid, they fought a fight that has never been set down in the newspapers. In response, many believe, to the fervent prayers of Father Dennis, the enemy not only elected to fight in the open, but made a beautiful fight, as many weeping Irish mothers knew later. They gathered behind walls or flickered across the open in shouting masses, and were pot-valiant in artillery. It was expedient to hold a large reserve and wait for the psychological moment that was being prepared by the shrieking shrapnel. Therefore the Mavericks lay down in open order on the brow of a hill to watch the play till their call should come. Father Dennis, whose duty was in the rear, to smooth the trouble of the wounded, had naturally managed to make his way to the foremost of his boys, and lay like a black porpoise, at length on the grass. To him crawled Mulcahy, ashen-gray, demanding absolution.

"Wait till you're shot," said Father Dennis sweetly. "There's a time for everything."

Dan Grady chuckled as he blew for the fiftieth time into the breech of his speckless rifle. Mulcahy groaned and buried his head in his arms till a stray shot spoke like a snipe immediately above his head, and a general heave and tremour rippled the line. Other shots followed and a few took effect, as a shriek or a grunt attested. The officers, who had been lying down with the men, rose and began to walk steadily up and down the front of their companies.

This manoeuvre, executed, not for publication, but as a guarantee of good faith, to soothe men, demands nerve. You must not hurry, you must not look nervous, though you know that you are a mark for every rifle within extreme range, and above all if you are smitten you must make as little noise as possible and roll inwards through the files. It is at this hour, when the breeze brings the first salt whiff of the powder to noses rather cold at the tip, and the eye can quietly take in the appearance of each red casualty, that the strain on the nerves is strongest. Scotch regiments can endure for half a day and abate no whit of their zeal at the end; English regiments sometimes sulk under punishment, while the Irish, like the French, are apt to run forward by ones and twos, which is just as bad as running back. The truly wise commandant of highly-strung troops allows them, in seasons of waiting, to hear the sound of their own voices uplifted in song. There is a legend of an English regiment that lay by its arms under fire chaunting "Sam Hall," to the horror of its newly appointed and pious colonel. The Black Boneens, who were suffering more than the Mavericks, on a hill half a mile away, began presently to explain to all who cared to listen—

We'll sound the jubilee, from the centre to the sea,

And Ireland shall be free, says the Shan-van Vogh.

"Sing, boys," said Father Dennis softly. "It looks as if we cared for their Afghan peas."

Dan Grady raised himself to his knees and opened his mouth in a song imparted to him, as to most of his comrades, in the strictest confidence by Mulcahy—that Mulcahy then lying limp and fainting on the grass, the chill fear of death upon him.

Company after company caught up the words which, the I. A. A. say, are to herald the general rising of Erin, and to breathe which, except to those duly appointed to hear, is death. Wherefore they are printed in this place.

The Saxon in Heaven's just balance is weighed,

His doom like Belshazzar's in death has been cast,

And the hand of the venger shall never be stayed

Till his race, faith, and speech are a dream of the past.

They were heart-filling lines and they ran with a swirl; the I. A. A. are better served by their pens than their petards. Dan clapped Mulcahy merrily on the back, asking him to sing up. The officers lay down again. There was no need to walk any more. Their men were soothing themselves thunderously, thus—

St. Mary in Heaven has written the vow

That the land shall not rest till the heretic blood,

From the babe at the breast to the hand at the plough,

Has rolled to the ocean like Shannon in flood!

"I'll speak to you after all's over," said Father Dennis authoritatively in Dan's ear. "What's the use of confessing to me when you do this foolishness? Dan, you've been playing with fire! I'll lay you more penance in a week than—"

"Come along to Purgatory with us, Father dear. The Boneens are on the move; they'll let us go now!"

The regiment rose to the blast of the bugle as one man; but one man there was who rose more swiftly than all the others, for half an inch of bayonet was in the fleshy part of his leg.

"You've got to do it," said Dan grimly. "Do it decent, anyhow;" and the roar of the rush drowned his words, for the rear companies thrust forward the first, still singing as they swung down the slope—

From the child at the breast to the hand at the plough

Shall roll to the ocean like Shannon in flood!

They should have sung it in the face of England, not of the Afghans, whom it impressed as much as did the wild Irish yell.

"They came down singing," said the unofficial report of the enemy, borne from village to village the next day. "They continued to sing, and it was written that our men could not abide when they came. It is believed that there was magic in the aforesaid song."

Dan and Horse Egan kept themselves in the neighbourhood of Mulcahy. Twice the man would have bolted back in the confusion. Twice he was heaved, kicked, and shouldered back again into the unpaintable inferno of a hotly contested charge.

At the end, the panic excess of his fear drove him into madness beyond all human courage. His eyes staring at nothing, his mouth open and frothing, and breathing as one in a cold bath, he went forward demented, while Dan toiled after him. The charge checked at a high mud wall. It was Mulcahy who scrambled up tooth and nail and hurled down among the bayonets the amazed Afghan who barred his way. It was Mulcahy, keeping to the straight line of the rabid dog, who led a collection of ardent souls at a newly unmasked battery and flung himself on the muzzle of a gun as his companions danced among the gunners. It was Mulcahy who ran wildly on from that battery into the open plain, where the enemy were retiring in sullen groups. His hands were empty, he had lost helmet and belt, and he was bleeding from a wound in the neck. Dan and Horse Egan, panting and distressed, had thrown themselves down on the ground by the captured guns, when they noticed Mulcahy's charge.

"Mad," said Horse Egan critically. "Mad with fear! He's going straight to his death, an' shouting's no use."

"Let him go. Watch now! If we fire we'll hit him maybe."

The last of a hurrying crowd of Afghans turned at the noise of shod feet behind him, and shifted his knife ready to hand. This, he saw, was no time to take prisoners. Mulcahy tore on, sobbing; the straight-held blade went home through the defenceless breast, and the body pitched forward almost before a shot from Dan's rifle brought down the slayer and still further hurried the Afghan retreat. The two Irishmen went out to bring in their dead.

"He was given the point, and that was an easy death," said Horse Egan, viewing the corpse. "But would you ha' shot him, Danny, if he had lived?"

"He didn't live, so there's no sayin'. But I doubt I wud have bekaze of the fun he gave us—let alone the beer. Hike up his legs, Horse, and we'll bring him in. Perhaps 'tis better this way."

They bore the poor limp body to the mass of the regiment, lolling open-mouthed on their rifles; and there was a general snigger when one of the younger subalterns said, "That was a good man!"

"Phew," said Horse Egan, when a burial-party had taken over the burden. "I'm powerful dhry, and this reminds me there'll be no more beer at all."

"Fwhy not?" said Dan, with a twinkle in his eye as he stretched himself for rest. "Are we not conspirin' all we can, an' while we conspire are we not entitled to free dhrinks? Sure his ould mother in New York would not let her son's comrades perish of drouth—if she can be reached at the end of a letter."

"You're a janius," said Horse Egan. "O' coorse she will not. I wish this crool war was over, an' we'd get back to canteen. Faith, the Commander-in-chief ought to be hanged in his own little sword-belt for makin' us work on wather."

The Mavericks were generally of Horse Egan's opinion. So they made haste to get their work done as soon as possible, and their industry was rewarded by unexpected peace. "We can fight the sons of Adam," said the tribesmen, "but we cannot fight the sons of Eblis, and this regiment never stays still in one place. Let us therefore come in." They came in, and "this regiment" withdrew to conspire under the leadership of Dan Grady.

Excellent as a subordinate, Dan failed altogether as a chief-in-command—possibly because he was too much swayed by the advice of the only man in the regiment who could manufacture more than one kind of handwriting. The same mail that bore to Mulcahy's mother in New York a letter from the colonel telling her how valiantly her son had fought for the

Queen, and how assuredly he would have been recommended for the Victoria Cross had he survived, carried a communication signed, I grieve to say, by that same colonel and all the officers of the regiment, explaining their willingness to do "anything which is contrary to the regulations and all kinds of revolutions" if only a little money could be forwarded to cover incidental expenses. Daniel Grady, Esquire, would receive funds, vice Mulcahy, who "was unwell at this present time of writing."

Both letters were forwarded from New York to Tehama Street, San Francisco, with marginal comments as brief as they were bitter. The Third Three read and looked at each other. Then the Second Conspirator—he who believed in "joining hands with the practical branches"—began to laugh, and on recovering his gravity said, "Gentlemen, I consider this will be a lesson to us. We're left again. Those cursed Irish have let us down. I knew they would, but"—here he laughed afresh—"I'd give considerable to know what was at the back of it all."

His curiosity would have been satisfied had he seen Dan Grady, discredited regimental conspirator, trying to explain to his thirsty comrades in India the non-arrival of funds from New York.

THE MAN WHO WAS

The Earth gave up her dead that tide,

Into our camp he came,

And said his say, and went his way,

And left our hearts aflame.

Keep tally—on the gun-butt score

The vengeance we must take,

When God shall bring full reckoning,

For our dead comrade's sake.

Ballad.

Let it be clearly understood that the Russian is a delightful person till he tucks in his shirt. As an Oriental he is charming. It is only when he insists upon being treated as the most easterly of western peoples instead of the most westerly of easterns that he becomes a racial anomaly extremely difficult to handle. The host never knows which side of his nature is going to turn up next.

Dirkovitch was a Russian—a Russian of the Russians—who appeared to get his bread by serving the Czar as an officer in a Cossack regiment, and corresponding for a Russian newspaper with a name that was never twice alike. He was a handsome young Oriental, fond of wandering through unexplored portions of the earth, and he arrived in India from nowhere in particular. At least no living man could ascertain whether it was by way of Balkh, Badakshan, Chitral, Beluchistan, or Nepaul, or anywhere else. The Indian Government, being in an unusually affable mood, gave orders that he was to be civilly treated and shown everything that was to be seen. So he drifted, talking bad English and worse French, from one city to another, till he foregathered with Her Majesty's White Hussars in the city of Peshawur, which stands at the mouth of that narrow swordcut in the hills that men call the Khyber Pass. He was undoubtedly an officer, and he was decorated after the manner of the Russians with little enamelled crosses, and he could talk, and (though this has nothing to do with his merits) he had been given up as a hopeless task, or cask, by the Black Tyrone, who individually and collectively, with hot whiskey and honey, mulled brandy, and mixed spirits of every kind, had striven in all hospitality to make him drunk. And when the Black Tyrone, who are exclusively Irish, fail to disturb the peace of head of a foreigner—that foreigner is certain to be a superior man.

The White Hussars were as conscientious in choosing their wine as in charging the enemy. All that they possessed, including some wondrous brandy, was placed at the absolute disposition of Dirkovitch, and he enjoyed himself hugely—even more than among the Black Tyrones.

But he remained distressingly European through it all. The White Hussars were "My dear true friends," "Fellow-soldiers glorious," and "Brothers inseparable." He would unburden himself by the hour on the glorious future that awaited the combined arms of England and Russia when their hearts and their territories should run side by side, and the great mission of civilising Asia should begin. That was unsatisfactory, because Asia is not going to be civilised after the methods of the West. There is too much Asia and she is too old. You cannot reform a lady of many lovers, and Asia has been insatiable in her flirtations aforetime. She will never attend Sunday-school or learn to vote save with swords for tickets.

Dirkovitch knew this as well as any one else, but it suited him to talk special-correspondently and to make himself as genial as he could. Now and then he volunteered a little, a very little, information about his own sotnia of Cossacks, left apparently to look after themselves somewhere at the back of beyond. He had done rough work in Central Asia, and had seen rather more help-yourself fighting than most men of his years. But he was careful never to betray his superiority, and more than careful to praise on all occasions the appearance, drill, uniform, and organisation of Her Majesty's White Hussars. And indeed they were a regiment to be admired. When Lady Durgan, widow of the late Sir John Durgan, arrived in their station, and after a short time had been proposed to by every single man at mess, she put the public sentiment very neatly when she explained that they were all so nice that unless she could marry them all, including the colonel and some majors already married, she was not going to content herself with one hussar. Wherefore she wedded a little man in a rifle regiment, being by nature contradictious; and the White Hussars were going to wear crape on their arms, but compromised by attending the wedding in full force, and lining the aisle with unutterable reproach. She had jilted them all—from Basset-Holmer the senior captain to little Mildred the junior subaltern, who could have given her four thousand a year and a title.

The only persons who did not share the general regard for the White Hussars were a few thousand gentlemen of Jewish extraction who lived across the border, and answered to the name of Pathan. They had once met the regiment officially and for something less than twenty minutes, but the interview, which was complicated with many casualties, had filled them with prejudice. They even called the White Hussars children of the devil and sons of persons whom it would be perfectly impossible to meet in decent society. Yet they were not above making their aversion fill their money-belts. The regiment possessed carbines—beautiful Martini-Henry carbines that would lob a bullet into an enemy's camp at one thousand yards, and were even handier than the long rifle. Therefore they were coveted all along the border, and since demand inevitably breeds supply, they were supplied at the risk of life and limb for exactly their weight in coined silver—seven and one half pounds' weight of rupees, or sixteen pounds sterling reckoning the rupee at par. They were stolen at night by snaky-haired thieves who crawled on their stomachs under the nose of the sentries; they disappeared mysteriously from locked arm-racks, and in the hot weather, when all the barrack doors and windows were open, they vanished like puffs of their own smoke. The border people desired them for family vendettas and contingencies. But in the long cold nights of the northern Indian winter they were stolen most extensively. The traffic of murder was liveliest among the hills at that season, and prices ruled high. The regimental guards were first doubled and then trebled. A trooper does not much care if he loses a weapon—Government must make it good—but he deeply resents the loss of his sleep. The regiment grew very angry, and one rifle-thief bears the visible marks of their anger upon him to this hour. That incident stopped the burglaries for a time, and the guards were reduced accordingly, and the regiment devoted itself to polo with unexpected results; for it beat by two goals to one that very terrible polo corps the Lushkar Light Horse, though the latter had four ponies apiece for a short hour's fight, as well as a native officer who played like a lambent flame across the ground.

They gave a dinner to celebrate the event. The Lushkar team came, and Dirkovitch came, in the fullest full uniform of a Cossack officer, which is as full as a dressing-gown, and was introduced to the Lushkars, and opened his eyes as he regarded. They were lighter men than the Hussars, and they carried themselves with the swing that is the peculiar right of the Punjab Frontier Force and all Irregular Horse. Like everything else in the Service it has to be learnt, but, unlike many things, it is never forgotten, and remains on the body till death.

The great beam-roofed mess-room of the White Hussars was a sight to be remembered. All the mess plate was out on the long table—the same table that had served up the bodies of five officers after a forgotten fight long and long ago—the dingy, battered standards faced the door of entrance, clumps of winter-roses lay between the silver candlesticks, and the portraits of eminent officers deceased looked down on their successors from between the heads of sambhur, nilghai, markhor, and, pride of all the mess, two grinning snow-leopards that had cost Basset-Holmer four months' leave that he might have spent in England, instead of on the road to Thibet and the daily risk of his life by ledge, snow-slide, and grassy slope.

The servants in spotless white muslin and the crest of their regiments on the brow of their turbans waited behind their masters, who were clad in the scarlet and gold of the White Hussars, and the cream and silver of the Lushkar Light Horse. Dirkovitch's dull green uniform was the only dark spot at the board, but his big onyx eyes made up for it. He was fraternising effusively with the captain of the Lushkar team, who was wondering how many of Dirkovitch's Cossacks his own dark wiry down-countrymen could account for in a fair charge. But one does not speak of these things openly.

The talk rose higher and higher, and the regimental band played between the courses, as is the immemorial custom, till all tongues ceased for a moment with the removal of the dinner-slips and the first toast of obligation, when an officer rising said, "Mr. Vice, the Queen," and little Mildred from the bottom of the table answered, "The Queen, God bless her," and the big spurs clanked as the big men heaved themselves up and drank the Queen upon whose pay they were falsely supposed to settle their mess-bills. That Sacrament of the Mess never grows old, and never ceases to bring a lump into the throat of the listener wherever he be by sea or by land. Dirkovitch rose with his "brothers glorious," but he could not understand. No one but an officer can tell what the toast means; and the bulk have more sentiment than comprehension. Immediately after the little silence that follows on the ceremony there entered the native officer who had played for the Lushkar team. He could not, of course, eat with the mess, but he came in at dessert, all six feet of him, with the blue and silver turban atop, and the big black boots below. The mess rose joyously as he thrust forward the hilt of his sabre in token of fealty for the colonel of the White Hussars to touch, and dropped into a vacant chair amid shouts of: "Rung ho, Hira Singh!" (which being translated means "Go in and win"). "Did I whack you over the knee, old man?" "Ressaidar Sahib, what the devil made you play that kicking pig of a pony in the last ten minutes?" "Shabash, Ressaidar Sahib!" Then the voice of the colonel, "The health of Ressaidar Hira Singh!"

After the shouting had died away Hira Singh rose to reply, for he was the cadet of a royal house, the son of a king's son, and knew what was due on these occasions. Thus he spoke in the vernacular:—"Colonel Sahib and officers of this regiment. Much honour have you done me. This will I remember. We came down from afar to play you. But we were beaten." ("No fault of yours, Ressaidar Sahib. Played on our own ground, y' know.

Your ponies were cramped from the railway. Don't apologise!") "Therefore perhaps we will come again if it be so ordained." ("Hear! Hear! Hear, indeed! Bravo! Hsh!") "Then we will play you afresh" ("Happy to meet you.") "till there are left no feet upon our ponies. Thus far for sport." He dropped one hand on his sword-hilt and his eye wandered to Dirkovitch lolling back in his chair. "But if by the will of God there arises any other game which is not the polo game, then be assured, Colonel Sahib and officers, that we will play it out side by side, though they," again his eye sought Dirkovitch, "though they, I say, have fifty ponies to our one horse." And with a deep-mouthed Rung ho! that sounded like a musket-butt on flagstones he sat down amid leaping glasses.

Dirkovitch, who had devoted himself steadily to the brandy—the terrible brandy aforementioned—did not understand, nor did the expurgated translations offered to him at all convey the point. Decidedly Hira Singh's was the speech of the evening, and the clamour might have continued to the dawn had it not been broken by the noise of a shot without that sent every man feeling at his defenseless left side. Then there was a scuffle and a yell of pain.

"Carbine-stealing again!" said the adjutant, calmly sinking back in his chair. "This comes of reducing the guards. I hope the sentries have killed him."

The feet of armed men pounded on the verandah flags, and it was as though something was being dragged.

"Why don't they put him in the cells till the morning?" said the colonel testily. "See if they've damaged him, sergeant."

The mess sergeant fled out into the darkness and returned with two troopers and a corporal, all very much perplexed.

"Caught a man stealin' carbines, sir," said the corporal. "Leastways 'e was crawlin' towards the barricks, sir, past the main road sentries, an' the sentry 'e sez, sir—"

The limp heap of rags upheld by the three men groaned. Never was seen so destitute and demoralised an Afghan. He was turbanless, shoeless, caked with dirt, and all but dead with rough handling. Hira Singh started slightly at the sound of the man's pain. Dirkovitch took another glass of brandy.

"What does the sentry say?" said the colonel.

"Sez 'e speaks English, sir," said the corporal.

"So you brought him into mess instead of handing him over to the sergeant! If he spoke all the Tongues of the Pentecost you've no business—"

Again the bundle groaned and muttered. Little Mildred had risen from his place to inspect. He jumped back as though he had been shot.

"Perhaps it would be better, sir, to send the men away," said he to the colonel, for he was a much privileged subaltern. He put his arms round the rag-bound horror as he spoke, and dropped him into a chair. It may not have been explained that the littleness of Mildred lay in his being six feet four and big in proportion. The corporal seeing that an officer was disposed to look after the capture, and that the colonel's eye was beginning to blaze, promptly removed himself and his men. The mess was left alone with the carbine-thief, who laid his head on the table and wept bitterly, hopelessly, and inconsolably as little children weep.

Hira Singh leapt to his feet. "Colonel Sahib," said he, "that man is no Afghan, for they weep Ai! Ai! Nor is he of Hindustan, for they weep Oh! Ho! He weeps after the fashion of the white men, who say Ow! Ow!"

"Now where the dickens did you get that knowledge, Hira Singh?" said the captain of the Lushkar team.

"Hear him!" said Hira Singh simply, pointing at the crumpled figure that wept as though it would never cease.

"He said, 'My God!'" said little Mildred. "I heard him say it."

The colonel and the mess-room looked at the man in silence. It is a horrible thing to hear a man cry. A woman can sob from the top—of her palate, or her lips, or anywhere else, but a man must cry from his diaphragm, and it rends him to pieces.

"Poor devil!" said the colonel, coughing tremendously. "We ought to send him to hospital. He's been man-handled."

Now the adjutant loved his carbines. They were to him as his grandchildren, the men standing in the first place. He grunted rebelliously: "I can understand an Afghan stealing, because he's built that way. But I can't understand his crying. That makes it worse."

The brandy must have affected Dirkovitch, for he lay back in his chair and stared at the ceiling. There was nothing special in the ceiling beyond a shadow as of a huge black coffin. Owing to some peculiarity in the construction of the mess-room, this shadow was always thrown when the candles were lighted. It never disturbed the digestion of the White Hussars. They were in fact rather proud of it.

"Is he going to cry all night?" said the colonel, "or are we supposed to sit up with little Mildred's guest until he feels better?"

The man in the chair threw up his head and stared at the mess. "Oh, my God!" he said, and every soul in the mess rose to his feet. Then the Lushkar captain did a deed for which he ought to have been given the Victoria Cross—distinguished gallantry in a fight against overwhelming curiosity. He picked up his team with his eyes as the hostess picks up the ladies at the opportune moment, and pausing only by the colonel's chair to say, "This isn't our affair, you know, sir," led them into the verandah and the gardens. Hira Singh was the last to go, and he looked at Dirkovitch. But Dirkovitch had departed into a brandy-paradise of his own. His lips moved without sound and he was studying the coffin on the ceiling.

"White—white all over," said Basset-Holmer, the adjutant. "What a pernicious renegade he must be! I wonder where he came from?"

The colonel shook the man gently by the arm, and "Who are you?" said he.

There was no answer. The man stared round the mess-room and smiled in the colonel's face. Little Mildred, who was always more of a woman than a man till "Boot and saddle" was sounded, repeated the question in a voice that would have drawn confidences from a geyser. The man only smiled. Dirkovitch at the far end of the table slid gently from his chair to the floor. No son of Adam in this present imperfect world can mix the Hussars' champagne with the Hussars' brandy by five and eight glasses of each without remembering the pit whence he was digged and descending thither. The band began to play the tune with which the White Hussars from the date of their formation have concluded all their functions. They would sooner be disbanded than abandon that tune; it is a part of their system. The man straightened himself in his chair and drummed on the table with his fingers.

"I don't see why we should entertain lunatics," said the colonel. "Call a guard and send him off to the cells. We'll look into the business in the morning. Give him a glass of wine first, though."

Little Mildred filled a sherry-glass with the brandy and thrust it over to the man. He drank, and the tune rose louder, and he straightened himself yet more. Then he put out his long-taloned hands to a piece of plate opposite and fingered it lovingly. There was a mystery connected with that piece of plate, in the shape of a spring which converted what was a seven-branched candlestick, three springs on each side and one in the middle, into a sort of wheel-spoke candelabrum. He found the spring, pressed it, and laughed weakly. He rose from his chair and inspected a picture on the wall, then moved on to another picture, the mess watching him without a word. When he came to the mantelpiece he shook his head and seemed distressed. A piece of plate representing a mounted hussar in full uniform caught his eye. He pointed to it, and then to the mantelpiece with inquiry in his eyes.

"What is it—Oh, what is it?" said little Mildred. Then as a mother might speak to a child, "That is a horse. Yes, a horse."

Very slowly came the answer in a thick, passionless guttural—"Yes, I—have seen. But—where is the horse?"

You could have heard the hearts of the mess beating as the men drew back to give the stranger full room in his wanderings. There was no question of calling the guard.

Again he spoke—very slowly, "Where is our horse?"

There is but one horse in the White Hussars, and his portrait hangs outside the door of the mess-room. He is the piebald drum-horse, the king of the regimental band, that served the regiment for seven-and-thirty years, and in the end was shot for old age. Half the mess tore the thing down from its place and thrust it into the man's hands. He placed it above the mantelpiece, it clattered on the ledge as his poor hands dropped it, and he staggered towards the bottom of the table, falling into Mildred's chair. Then all the men spoke to one another something after this fashion, "The drum-horse hasn't hung over the mantelpiece since '67." "How does he know?" "Mildred, go and speak to him again." "Colonel, what are you going to do?" "Oh, dry up, and give the poor devil a chance to pull himself together." "It isn't possible anyhow. The man's a lunatic."

Little Mildred stood at the colonel's side, talking in his ear. "Will you be good enough to take your seats please, gentlemen!" he said, and the mess dropped into the chairs. Only Dirkovitch's seat, next to little Mildred's, was blank, and little Mildred himself had found Hira Singh's place. The wide-eyed mess-sergeant filled the glasses in dead silence. Once more the colonel rose, but his hand shook, and the port spilled on the table as he looked straight at the man in little Mildred's chair and said hoarsely, "Mr. Vice, the Queen." There was a little pause, but the man sprung to his feet and answered without hesitation, "The Queen, God bless her!" and as he emptied the thin glass he snapped the shank between his fingers.

Long and long ago, when the Empress of India was a young woman, and there were no unclean ideals in the land, it was the custom of a few messes to drink the Queen's toast in broken glass, to the vast delight of the mess-contractors. The custom is now dead, because there is nothing to break anything for, except now and again the word of a Government, and that has been broken already.

"That settles it," said the colonel, with a gasp. "He's not a sergeant. What in the world is he?"

The entire mess echoed the word, and the volley of questions would have scared any man. It was no wonder that the ragged, filthy invader could only smile and shake his head.

From under the table, calm and smiling, rose Dirkovitch, who had been roused from healthful slumber by feet upon his body. By the side of the man he rose, and the man shrieked and grovelled. It was a horrible sight, coming so swiftly upon the pride and glory of the toast that had brought the strayed wits together.

Dirkovitch made no offer to raise him, but little Mildred heaved him up in an instant. It is not good that a gentleman who can answer to the Queen's toast should lie at the feet of a subaltern of Cossacks.

The hasty action tore the wretch's upper clothing nearly to the waist, and his body was seamed with dry black scars. There is only one weapon in the world that cuts in parallel lines, and it is neither the cane nor the cat. Dirkovitch saw the marks, and the pupils of his eyes dilated. Also his face changed. He said something that sounded like Shto ve takete, and the man fawning answered, Chetyre.

"What's that?" said everybody together.

"His number. That is number four, you know." Dirkovitch spoke very thickly.

"What has a Queen's officer to do with a qualified number?" said the Colonel, and an unpleasant growl ran round the table.

"How can I tell?" said the affable Oriental with a sweet smile. "He is a—how you have it?—escape—run-a-way, from over there." He nodded towards the darkness of the night.

"Speak to him if he'll answer you, and speak to him gently," said little Mildred, settling the man in a chair. It seemed most improper to all present that Dirkovitch should sip brandy as he talked in purring, spitting Russian to the creature who answered so feebly and with such evident dread. But since Dirkovitch appeared to understand, no one said a word. All breathed heavily, leaning forward, in the long gaps of the conversation. The next time that they have no engagements on hand the White Hussars intend to go to St. Petersburg in a body to learn Russian.

"He does not know how many years ago," said Dirkovitch, facing the mess, "but he says it was very long ago in a war. I think that there was an accident. He says he was of this glorious and distinguished regiment in the war."

"The rolls! The rolls! Holmer, get the rolls!" said little Mildred, and the adjutant dashed off bare-headed to the orderly-room, where the muster-rolls of the regiment were kept. He returned just in time to hear Dirkovitch conclude, "Therefore, my dear friends, I am most sorry to say there was an accident which would have been reparable if he had apologised to that our colonel, which he had insulted."

Then followed another growl which the colonel tried to beat down. The mess was in no mood just then to weigh insults to Russian colonels.

"He does not remember, but I think that there was an accident, and so he was not exchanged among the prisoners, but he was sent to another place—how do you say?—the country. So, he says, he came here. He does not know how he came. Eh? He was at Chepany,"—the man caught the word, nodded, and shivered,—"at Zhigansk and Irkutsk. I cannot understand how he escaped. He says, too, that he was in the forests for many years, but how many years he has forgotten—that with many things. It was an accident; done because he did not apologise to that our colonel. Ah!"

Instead of echoing Dirkovitch's sigh of regret, it is sad to record that the White Hussars livelily exhibited un-Christian delight and other emotions, hardly restrained by their sense of hospitality. Holmer flung the frayed and yellow regimental rolls on the table, and the men flung themselves at these.

"Steady! Fifty-six—fifty-five—fifty-four," said Holmer. "Here we are. 'Lieutenant Austin Limmason. Missing.' That was before Sebastopol. What an infernal shame! Insulted one of their colonels, and was quietly shipped off. Thirty years of his life wiped out."

"But he never apologised. Said he'd see him damned first," chorused the mess.

"Poor chap! I suppose he never had the chance afterwards. How did he come here?" said the colonel.

The dingy heap in the chair could give no answer.

"Do you know who you are?"

It laughed weakly.

"Do you know that you are Limmason—Lieutenant Limmason of the White Hussars?"

Swiftly as a shot came the answer, in a slightly surprised tone, "Yes, I'm—Limmason, of course." The light died out in his eyes, and the man collapsed, watching every motion of Dirkovitch with terror. A flight from Siberia may fix a few elementary facts in the mind, but it does not seem to lead to continuity of thought. The man could not explain how, like a homing pigeon, he had found his way to his own old mess again. Of what he had suffered or seen he knew nothing. He cringed before Dirkovitch as instinctively as he had pressed the spring of the candlestick, sought the picture of the drum-horse, and answered to the toast of the Queen. The rest was a blank that the dreaded Russian tongue could only in part remove. His head bowed on his breast, and he giggled and cowered alternately.

The devil that lived in the brandy prompted Dirkovitch at this extremely inopportune moment to make a speech. He rose, swaying slightly, gripped the table-edge, while his eyes glowed like opals, and began:

"Fellow-soldiers glorious—true friends and hospitables. It was an accident, and deplorable—most deplorable." Here he smiled sweetly all round the mess. "But you will think of this little, little thing. So little, is it not? The Czar! Posh! I slap my fingers—I snap my fingers at him. Do I believe in him? No! But in us Slav who has done nothing, him I believe. Seventy—how much—millions peoples that have done nothing—not one thing. Posh! Napoleon was an episode." He banged a hand on the table. "Hear you, old peoples, we have done nothing in the world—out here. All our work is to do; and it shall be done, old peoples. Get a-way!" He waved his hand imperiously, and pointed to the man. "You see him. He is not good to see. He was just one little—oh, so little—accident, that no one remembered. Now he is——"

"That! So will you be, brother soldiers so brave so will you be. But you will never come back. You will all go where he is gone, or"—he pointed to the great coffin-shadow on the ceiling, and muttering, "Seventy millions—get a-way, you old peoples," fell asleep.

"Sweet, and to the point," said little Mildred. "What's the use of getting wroth? Let's make this poor devil comfortable."

But that was a matter suddenly and swiftly taken from the loving hands of the White Hussars. The lieutenant had returned only to go away again three days later, when the wail of the Dead March, and the tramp of the squadrons, told the wondering Station, who saw no gap in the mess-table, that an officer of the regiment had resigned his new-found commission.

And Dirkovitch, bland, supple, and always genial, went away too by a night train. Little Mildred and another man saw him off, for he was the guest of the mess, and even had he smitten the colonel with the open hand, the law of that mess allowed no relaxation of hospitality.

"Good-bye, Dirkovitch, and a pleasant journey," said little Mildred.

"Au revoir," said the Russian.

"Indeed! But we thought you were going home?"

"Yes, but I will come again. My dear friends, is that road shut?" He pointed to where the North Star burned over the Khyber Pass.

"By Jove! I forgot. Of course. Happy to meet you, old man, any time you like. Got everything you want? Cheroots, ice, bedding? That's all right. Well, au revoir, Dirkovitch."

"Um," said the other man, as the tail-lights of the train grew small. "Of—all—the—unmitigated!"

Little Mildred answered nothing, but watched the North Star and hummed a selection from recent Simla burlesque that had much delighted the White Hussars. It ran—

> *I'm sorry for Mister Bluebeard,*
>
> *I'm sorry to cause him pain;*
>
> *But a terrible spree there's sure to be*
>
> *When he comes back again.*

ONLY A SUBALTERN

*Not only to enforce by command but to encourage by example
the energetic discharge of duty and the steady endurance of
the difficulties and privations inseparable from Military
Service.—Bengal Army Regulations.*

They made Bobby Wick pass an examination at Sandhurst. He was a
gentleman before he was gazetted, so, when the Empress announced that
"Gentleman-Cadet Robert Hanna Wick" was posted as Second Lieutenant
to the Tyneside Tail Twisters at Krab Bokhar, he became an officer and a
gentleman, which is an enviable thing; and there was joy in the house of
Wick, where Mamma Wick and all the little Wicks fell upon their knees and
offered incense to Bobby by virtue of his achievements.

Papa Wick had been a Commissioner in his day, holding authority over
three millions of men in the Chota-Buldana Division, building great works
for the good of the land, and doing his best to make two blades of grass
grow where there was but one before. Of course, nobody knew anything
about this in the little English village where he was just "old Mr. Wick" and
had forgotten that he was a Companion of the Order of the Star of India.

He patted Bobby on the shoulder and said: "Well done, my boy!"

There followed, while the uniform was being prepared, an interval of
pure delight, during which Bobby took brevet-rank as a "man" at the
women-swamped tennis-parties and tea-fights of the village, and, I daresay,
had his joining-time been extended, would have fallen in love with several
girls at once. Little country villages at Home are very full of nice girls,
because all the young men come out to India to make their fortunes.

"India," said Papa Wick, "is the place. I've had thirty years of it, and,
begad, I'd like to go back again. When you join the Tail Twisters you'll be
among friends, if every one hasn't forgotten Wick of Chota-Buldana, and a
lot of people will be kind to you for our sakes. The mother will tell you
more about outfit than I can, but remember this. Stick to your Regiment,
Bobby—stick to your Regiment. You'll see men all round you going into
the Staff Corps, and doing every possible sort of duty but regimental, and
you may be tempted to follow suit. Now so long as you keep within your
allowance, and I haven't stinted you there, stick to the Line, the whole Line,
and nothing but the Line. Be careful how you back another young fool's

- 56 -

bill, and if you fall in love with a woman twenty years older than yourself, don't tell me about it, that's all."

With these counsels, and many others equally valuable, did Papa Wick fortify Bobby ere that last awful night at Portsmouth when the Officers' Quarters held more inmates than were provided for by the Regulations, and the liberty-men of the ships fell foul of the drafts for India, and the battle raged from the Dockyard Gates even to the slums of Longport, while the drabs of Fratton came down and scratched the faces of the Queen's Officers.

Bobby Wick, with an ugly bruise on his freckled nose, a sick and shaky detachment to manoeuvre inship, and the comfort of fifty scornful females to attend to, had no time to feel homesick till the Malabar reached mid-Channel, when he doubled his emotions with a little guard-visiting and a great many other matters.

The Tail Twisters were a most particular Regiment. Those who knew them least said that they were eaten up with "side." But their reserve and their internal arrangements generally were merely protective diplomacy. Some five years before, the Colonel commanding had looked into the fourteen fearless eyes of seven plump and juicy subalterns who had all applied to enter the Staff Corps, and had asked them why the three stars should he, a colonel of the Line, command a dashed nursery for double-dashed bottle-suckers who put on condemned tin spurs and rode qualified mokes at the hiatused heads of forsaken Black Regiments. He was a rude man and a terrible. Wherefore the remnant took measures (with the half-butt as an engine of public opinion) till the rumour went abroad that young men who used the Tail Twisters as a crutch to the Staff Corps had many and varied trials to endure. However, a regiment has just as much right to its own secrets as a woman.

When Bobby came up from Deolali and took his place among the Tail Twisters, it was gently but firmly borne in upon him that the Regiment was his father and his mother and his indissolubly wedded wife, and that there was no crime under the canopy of heaven blacker than that of bringing shame on the Regiment, which was the best-shooting, best-drilled, best set-up, bravest, most illustrious, and in all respects most desirable Regiment within the compass of the Seven Seas. He was taught the legends of the Mess Plate, from the great grinning Golden Gods that had come out of the Summer Palace in Pekin to the silver-mounted markhor-horn snuffmull presented by the last C. O. (he who spake to the seven subalterns). And every one of those legends told him of battles fought at long odds, without fear as without support; of hospitality catholic as an Arab's; of friendships deep as the sea and steady as the fighting-line; of honour won by hard roads for honour's sake; and of instant and unquestioning devotion to the Regiment—the Regiment that claims the lives of all and lives forever.

More than once, too, he came officially into contact with the Regimental colours, which looked like the lining of a bricklayer's hat on the end of a chewed stick. Bobby did not kneel and worship them, because British subalterns are not constructed in that manner. Indeed, he condemned them for their weight at the very moment that they were filling him with awe and other more noble sentiments.

But best of all was the occasion when he moved with the Tail Twisters in review order at the breaking of a November day. Allowing for duty-men and sick, the Regiment was one thousand and eighty strong, and Bobby belonged to them; for was he not a Subaltern of the Line,—the whole Line and nothing but the Line,—as the tramp of two thousand one hundred and sixty sturdy ammunition boots attested? He would not have changed places with Deighton of the Horse Battery, whirling by in a pillar of cloud to a chorus of "Strong right! Strong left!" or Hogan-Yale of the White Hussars, leading his squadron for all it was worth, with the price of horseshoes thrown in; or "Tick" Boileau, trying to live up to his fierce blue and gold turban while the wasps of the Bengal Cavalry stretched to a gallop in the wake of the long, lollopping Walers of the White Hussars.

They fought through the clear cool day, and Bobby felt a little thrill run down his spine when he heard the tinkle-tinkle-tinkle of the empty cartridge-cases hopping from the breech-blocks after the roar of the volleys; for he knew that he should live to hear that sound in action. The review ended in a glorious chase across the plain—batteries thundering after cavalry to the huge disgust of the White Hussars, and the Tyneside Tail Twisters hunting a Sikh Regiment till the lean, lathy Singhs panted with exhaustion. Bobby was dusty and dripping long before noon, but his enthusiasm was merely focused—not diminished.

He returned to sit at the feet of Revere, his "skipper," that is to say, the Captain of his Company, and to be instructed in the dark art and mystery of managing men, which is a very large part of the Profession of Arms.

"If you haven't a taste that way," said Revere between his puffs of his cheroot, "you'll never be able to get the hang of it, but remember, Bobby, 'tisn't the best drill, though drill is nearly everything, that hauls a Regiment through Hell and out on the other side. It's the man who knows how to handle men—goat-men, swine-men, dog-men, and so on."

"Dormer, for instance," said Bobby; "I think he comes under the head of fool-men. He mopes like a sick owl."

"That's where you make your mistake, my son. Dormer isn't a fool yet, but he's a dashed dirty soldier, and his room corporal makes fun of his socks before kit-inspection. Dormer, being two-thirds pure brute, goes into a corner and growls."

"How do you know'?" said Bobby admiringly.

"Because a Company commander has to know these things—because, if he does not know, he may have crime—ay, murder—brewing under his very nose and yet not see that it's there. Dormer is being badgered out of his mind—big as he is—and he hasn't intellect enough to resent it. He's taken to quiet boozing, and, Bobby, when the butt of a room goes on the drink, or takes to moping by himself, measures are necessary to pull him out of himself."

"What measures? Man can't run round coddling his men for ever."

"No. The men would precious soon show him that he was not wanted. You've got to—"

Here the Colour-sergeant entered with some papers; Bobby reflected for a while as Revere looked through the Company forms.

"Does Dormer do anything, Sergeant?" Bobby asked with the air of one continuing an interrupted conversation.

"No, sir. Does 'is dooty like a hortomato," said the Sergeant, who delighted in long words. "A dirty soldier, and 'e's under full stoppages for new kit. It's covered with scales, sir."

"Scales? What scales?"

"Fish-scales, sir. 'E's always pokin' in the mud by the river an' a-cleanin' them muchly-fish with 'is thumbs." Revere was still absorbed in the Company papers, and the Sergeant, who was sternly fond of Bobby, continued,—"'E generally goes down there when 'e's got 'is skinful, beggin' your pardon, sir, an' they do say that the more lush—inebriated 'e is, the more fish 'e catches. They call 'im the Looney Fishmonger in the Comp'ny, sir."

Revere signed the last paper and the Sergeant retreated.

"It's a filthy amusement," sighed Bobby to himself. Then aloud to Revere: "Are you really worried about Dormer?"

"A little. You see he's never mad enough to send to hospital, or drunk enough to run in, but at any minute he may flare up, brooding and sulking as he does. He resents any interest being shown in him, and the only time I took him out shooting he all but shot me by accident."

"I fish," said Bobby, with a wry face. "I hire a country-boat and go down river from Thursday to Sunday, and the amiable Dormer goes with me—if you can spare us both."

"You blazing young fool!" said Revere, but his heart was full of much more pleasant words.

Bobby, the Captain of a dhoni, with Private Dormer for mate, dropped down the river on Thursday morning—the Private at the bow, the Subaltern at the helm. The Private glared uneasily at the Subaltern, who respected the reserve of the Private.

After six hours, Dormer paced to the stern, saluted, and said—"Beg y' pardon, sir, but was you ever on the Durh'm Canal?"

"No," said Bobby Wick. "Come and have some tiffin."

They ate in silence. As the evening fell, Private Dormer broke forth, speaking to himself—

"Hi was on the Durh'm Canal, jes' such a night, come next week twelvemonth, a-trailin' of my toes in the water." He smoked and said no more till bedtime.

The witchery of the dawn turned the gray river-reaches to purple, gold, and opal; and it was as though the lumbering dhoni crept across the splendours of a new heaven.

Private Dormer popped his head out of his blanket and gazed at the glory below and around.

"Well—damn—my eyes!" said Private Dormer in an awed whisper. "This 'ere is like a bloomin' gallantry-show!" For the rest of the day he was dumb, but achieved an ensanguined filthiness through the cleaning of big fish.

The boat returned on Saturday evening. Dormer had been struggling with speech since noon. As the lines and luggage were being disembarked, he found tongue.

"Beg y' pardon, sir," he said, "but would you—would you min' shakin' 'ands with me, sir?"

"Of course not," said Bobby, and he shook accordingly. Dormer returned to barracks and Bobby to mess.

"He wanted a little quiet and some fishing, I think," said Bobby. "My aunt, but he's a filthy sort of animal! Have you ever seen him clean 'them muchly-fish with 'is thumbs?"

"Anyhow," said Revere three weeks later, "he's doing his best to keep his things clean."

When the spring died, Bobby joined in the general scramble for Hill leave, and to his surprise and delight secured three months.

"As good a boy as I want," said Revere, the admiring skipper.

"The best of the batch," said the Adjutant to the Colonel. "Keep back that young skrimshanker Porkiss, sir, and let Revere make him sit up."

So Bobby departed joyously to Simla Pahar with a tin box of gorgeous raiment.

"Son of Wick—old Wick of Chota-Buldana? Ask him to dinner, dear," said the aged men.

"What a nice boy!" said the matrons and the maids.

"First-class place, Simla. Oh, ri——ipping!" said Bobby Wick, and ordered new white cord breeches on the strength of it.

"We're in a bad way," wrote Revere to Bobby at the end of two months. "Since you left, the Regiment has taken to fever and is fairly rotten with it—two hundred in hospital, about a hundred in cells—drinking to keep off fever—and the Companies on parade fifteen file strong at the outside. There's rather more sickness in the out-villages than I care for, but then I'm so blistered with prickly-heat that I'm ready to hang myself. What's the yarn about your mashing a Miss Haverley up there? Not serious, I hope? You're over-young to hang millstones round your neck, and the Colonel will turf you out of that in double-quick time if you attempt it."

It was not the Colonel that brought Bobby out of Simla, but a much more to be respected Commandant. The sickness in the out-villages spread, the Bazar was put out of bounds, and then came the news that the Tail Twisters must go into camp. The message flashed to the Hill stations.— "Cholera—Leave stopped—Officers recalled." Alas, for the white gloves in the neatly soldered boxes, the rides and the dances and picnics that were to be, the loves half spoken, and the debts unpaid! Without demur and without question, fast as tonga could fly or pony gallop, back to their Regiments and their Batteries, as though they were hastening to their weddings, fled the subalterns.

Bobby received his orders on returning from a dance at Viceregal Lodge, where he had but only the Haverley girl knows what Bobby had said or how many waltzes he had claimed for the next ball. Six in the morning saw Bobby at the Tonga Office in the drenching rain, the whirl of the last waltz still in his ears, and an intoxication due neither to wine nor waltzing in his brain.

"Good man!" shouted Deighton of the Horse Battery through the mists. "Whar you raise dat tonga? I'm coming with you. Ow! But I've a head and half. I didn't sit out all night. They say the Battery's awful bad," and he hummed dolorously—

"Leave the what at the what's-its-name,

Leave the flock without shelter,

Leave the corpse uninterred,

Leave the bride at the altar

"My faith! It'll be more bally corpse than bride, though, this journey. Jump in, Bobby. Get on, Coachwan!"

On the Umballa platform waited a detachment of officers discussing the latest news from the stricken cantonment, and it was here that Bobby learned the real condition of the Tail Twisters.

"They went into camp," said an elderly Major recalled from the whist-tables at Mussoorie to a sickly Native Regiment, "they went into camp with two hundred and ten sick in carts. Two hundred and ten fever cases only, and the balance looking like so many ghosts with sore eyes. A Madras Regiment could have walked through 'em."

"But they were as fit as be-damned when I left them!" said Bobby.

"Then you'd better make them as fit as be-damned when you rejoin," said the Major brutally.

Bobby pressed his forehead against the rain-splashed window-pane as the train lumbered across the sodden Doab, and prayed for the health of the Tyneside Tail Twisters. Naini Tal had sent down her contingent with all speed; the lathering ponies of the Dalhousie Road staggered into Pathankot, taxed to the full stretch of their strength; while from cloudy Darjiling the Calcutta Mail whirled up the last straggler of the little army that was to fight a fight, in which was neither medal nor honour for the winning, against an enemy none other than "the sickness that destroyeth in the noonday."

And as each man reported himself, he said: "This is a bad business," and went about his own forthwith, for every Regiment and Battery in the cantonment was under canvas, the sickness bearing them company.

Bobby fought his way through the rain to the Tail Twisters' temporary mess, and Revere could have fallen on the boy's neck for the joy of seeing that ugly, wholesome phiz once more.

"Keep 'em amused and interested," said Revere. "They went on the drink, poor fools, after the first two cases, and there was no improvement. Oh, it's good to have you back, Bobby! Porkiss is a—never mind."

Deighton came over from the Artillery camp to attend a dreary mess dinner, and contributed to the general gloom by nearly weeping over the condition of his beloved Battery. Porkiss so far forgot himself as to insinuate that the presence of the officers could do no earthly good, and that the best thing would be to send the entire Regiment into hospital and "let the doctors look after them." Porkiss was demoralised with fear, nor was his peace of mind restored when Revere said coldly: "Oh! The sooner you go out the better, if that's your way of thinking. Any public school could send us fifty good men in your place, but it takes time, time, Porkiss, and money, and a certain amount of trouble, to make a Regiment. S'pose you're the person we go into camp for, eh?"

Whereupon Porkiss was overtaken with a great and chilly fear which a drenching in the rain did not allay, and, two days later, quitted this world for another where, men do fondly hope, allowances are made for the weaknesses of the flesh. The Regimental Sergeant-Major looked wearily across the Sergeants' Mess tent when the news was announced.

"There goes the worst of them," he said. "It'll take the best, and then, please God, it'll stop." The Sergeants were silent till one said: "It couldn't be him!" and all knew of whom Travis was thinking.

Bobby Wick stormed through the tents of his Company, rallying, rebuking, mildly, as is consistent with the Regulations, chaffing the fainthearted; haling the sound into the watery sunlight when there was a break in the weather, and bidding them be of good cheer, for their trouble was nearly at an end; scuttling on his dun pony round the outskirts of the camp and heading back men who, with the innate perversity of British soldiers, were always wandering into infected villages, or drinking deeply from rain-flooded marshes; comforting the panic-stricken with rude speech, and more than once tending the dying who had no friends—the men without "townies"; organizing, with banjos and burnt cork, Sing-songs which should allow the talent of the Regiment full play; and generally, as he explained, "playing the giddy garden-goat all round."

"You're worth half a dozen of us, Bobby," said Revere in a moment of enthusiasm. "How the devil do you keep it up?"

Bobby made no answer, but had Revere looked into the breast-pocket of his coat he might have seen there a sheaf of badly-written letters which perhaps accounted for the power that possessed the boy. A letter came to Bobby every other day. The spelling was not above reproach, but the sentiments must have been most satisfactory, for on receipt Bobby's eyes softened marvellously, and he was wont to fall into a tender abstraction for a while ere, shaking his cropped head, he charged into his work.

By what power he drew after him the hearts of the roughest, and the Tail Twisters counted in their ranks some rough diamonds indeed, was a mystery to both skipper and C. O., who learned from the regimental chaplain that Bobby was considerably more in request in the hospital tents than the Reverend John Emery.

"The men seem fond of you. Are you in the hospitals much?" said the Colonel, who did his daily round and ordered the men to get well with a hardness that did not cover his bitter grief.

"A little, sir," said Bobby.

"Shouldn't go there too often if I were you. They say it's not contagious, but there's no use in running unnecessary risks. We can't afford to have you down, y' know."

Six days later, it was with the utmost difficulty that the post-runner plashed his way out to the camp with the mail-bags, for the rain was falling in torrents. Bobby received a letter, bore it off to his tent, and, the programme for the next week's Sing-song being satisfactorily disposed of, sat down to answer it. For an hour the unhandy pen toiled over the paper, and where sentiment rose to more than normal tide-level, Bobby Wick stuck out his tongue and breathed heavily. He was not used to letter-writing.

"Beg y' pardon, sir," said a voice at the tent door; "but Dormer's 'orrid bad, sir, an' they've taken him orf, sir."

"Damn Private Dormer and you too!" said Bobby Wick, running the blotter over the half-finished letter. "Tell him I'll come in the morning."

"'E's awful bad, sir," said the voice hesitatingly. There was an undecided squelching of heavy boots.

"Well?" said Bobby impatiently.

"Excusin' 'imself before 'and for takin' the liberty, 'e says it would be a comfort for to assist 'im, sir, if—tattoo lao! Get my pony! Here, come in out of the rain till I'mready. What blasted nuisances you are! That's brandy.

Drink some; you want it. Hang on to my stirrup and tell me if I go too fast."

Strengthened by a four-finger "nip" which he swallowed without a wink, the Hospital Orderly kept up with the slipping, mud-stained, and very disgusted pony as it shambled to the hospital tent.

Private Dormer was certainly "'orrid bad." He had all but reached the stage of collapse, and was not pleasant to look upon.

"What's this, Dormer?" said Bobby, bending over the man. "You're not going out this time. You've got to come fishing with me once or twice more yet."

The blue lips parted and in the ghost of a whisper said,—"Beg y' pardon, sir, disturbin' of you now, but would you min' 'oldin' my 'and, sir'?"

Bobby sat on the side of the bed, and the icy-cold hand closed on his own like a vice, forcing a lady's ring which was on the little finger deep into the flesh. Bobby set his lips and waited, the water dripping from the hem of his trousers. An hour passed, and the grasp of the hand did not relax, nor did the expression of the drawn face change. Bobby with infinite craft lit himself a cheroot with the left hand (his right arm was numbed to the elbow), and resigned himself to a night of pain.

Dawn showed a very white-faced Subaltern sitting on the side of a sick man's cot, and a Doctor in the doorway using language unfit for publication.

"Have you been here all night, you young ass?" said the Doctor.

"There or thereabouts," said Bobby ruefully. "He's frozen on to me."

Dormer's mouth shut with a click. He turned his head and sighed. The clinging hand opened, and Bobby's arm fell useless at his side.

"He'll do," said the Doctor quietly. "It must have been a toss-up all through the night. 'Think you're to be congratulated on this case."

"Oh, bosh!" said Bobby. "I thought the man had gone out long ago—only—only I didn't care to take my hand away. Rub my arm down, there's a good chap. What a grip the brute has! I'm chilled to the marrow!" He passed out of the tent shivering.

Private Dormer was allowed to celebrate his repulse of Death by strong waters. Four days later, he sat on the side of his cot and said to the patients mildly: "I'd 'a' liken to 'a' spoken to 'im—so I should."

But at that time Bobby was reading yet another letter,—he had the most persistent correspondent of any man in camp,—and was even then about to write that the sickness had abated, and in another week at the outside would be gone. He did not intend to say that the chill of a sick man's hand seemed to have struck into the heart whose capacities for affection he dwelt on at such length. He did intend to enclose the illustrated programme of the forthcoming Sing-song, whereof he was not a little proud. He also intended to write on many other matters which do not concern us, and doubtless would have done so but for the slight feverish headache which made him dull and unresponsive at mess.

"You are overdoing it, Bobby," said his skipper. "Might give the rest of us credit of doing a little work. You go on as if you were the whole Mess rolled into one. Take it easy."

"I will," said Bobby. "I'm feeling done up, somehow." Revere looked at him anxiously and said nothing.

There was a flickering of lanterns about the camp that night, and a rumour that brought men out of their cots to the tent doors, a paddling of the naked feet of doolie-bearers, and the rush of a galloping horse.

"Wot's up?" asked twenty tents; and through twenty tents ran the answer—"Wick, 'e's down."

They brought the news to Revere and he groaned. "Any one but Bobby and I shouldn't have cared! The Sergeant-Major was right."

"Not going out this journey," gasped Bobby, as he was lifted from the doolie. "Not going out this journey." Then with an air of supreme conviction—"I can't, you see."

"Not if I can do anything!" said the Surgeon-Major, who had hastened over from the mess where he had been dining.

He and the Regimental Surgeon fought together with Death for the life of Bobby Wick. Their work was interrupted by a hairy apparition in a blue-gray dressing-gown, who stared in horror at the bed and cried—"Oh, my Gawd! It can't be 'im!" until an indignant Hospital Orderly whisked him away.

If care of man and desire to live could have done aught, Bobby would have been saved. As it was, he made a fight of three days, and the Surgeon-Major's brow uncreased. "We'll save him yet," he said; and the Surgeon, who, though he ranked with the Captain, had a very youthful heart, went out upon the word and pranced joyously in the mud.

"Not going out this journey," whispered Bobby Wick gallantly, at the end of the third day.

"Bravo!" said the Surgeon-Major. "That's the way to look at it, Bobby."

As evening fell a gray shade gathered round Bobby's mouth, and he turned his face to the tent-wall wearily. The Surgeon-Major frowned.

"I'm awfully tired," said Bobby, very faintly. "What's the use of bothering me with medicine? I—don't—want—it. Let me alone."

The desire for life had departed, and Bobby was content to drift away on the easy tide of Death.

"It's no good," said the Surgeon-Major. "He doesn't want to live. He's meeting it, poor child." And he blew his nose.

Half a mile away, the regimental band was playing the overture to the Sing-song, for the men had been told that Bobby was out of danger. The clash of the brass and the wail of the horns reached Bobby's ears.

> *Is there a single joy or pain,*
>
> *That I should never kno-ow?*
>
> *You do not love me, 'tis in vain,*
>
> *Bid me good-bye and go!*

An expression of hopeless irritation crossed the boy's face, and he tried to shake his head.

The Surgeon-Major bent down—"What is it, Bobby?"—-"Not that waltz," muttered Bobby. "That's our own—our very ownest own... Mummy dear."

With this he sank into the stupor that gave place to death early next morning.

Revere, his eyes red at the rims and his nose very white, went into Bobby's tent to write a letter to Papa Wick which should bow the white head of the ex-Commissioner of Chota-Buldana in the keenest sorrow of his life. Bobby's little store of papers lay in confusion on the table, and among them a half-finished letter. The last sentence ran: "So you see, darling, there is really no fear, because as long as I know you care for me and I care for you, nothing can touch me."

Revere stayed in the tent for an hour. When he came out, his eyes were redder than ever.

Private Conklin sat on a turned-down bucket, and listened to a not unfamiliar tune. Private Conklin was a convalescent and should have been tenderly treated.

"Ho!" said Private Conklin. "There's another bloomin' orf'cer da-ed."

The bucket shot from under him, and his eyes filled with a smithyful of sparks. A tall man in a blue-gray bedgown was regarding him with deep disfavour.

"You ought to take shame for yourself, Conky! Orf'cer?—bloomin' orf'cer? I'll learn you to misname the likes of 'im. Hangel! Bloomin' Hangel! That's wot 'e is!"

And the Hospital Orderly was so satisfied with the justice of the punishment that he did not even order Private Dormer back to his cot.

IN THE MATTER OF A PRIVATE

Hurrah! hurrah! a soldier's life for me!
Shout, boys, shout! for it makes you jolly and free.

The Ramrod Corps.

People who have seen say that one of the quaintest spectacles of human frailty is an outbreak of hysterics in a girls' school. It starts without warning, generally on a hot afternoon, among the elder pupils. A girl giggles till the giggle gets beyond control. Then she throws up her head and cries, "Honk, honk, honk," like a wild goose, and tears mix with the laughter. If the mistress be wise, she will rap out something severe at this point to check matters. If she be tender-hearted, and send for a drink of water, the chances are largely in favour of another girl laughing at the afflicted one and herself collapsing. Thus the trouble spreads, and may end in half of what answers to the Lower Sixth of a boys' school rocking and whooping together. Given a week of warm weather, two stately promenades per diem, a heavy mutton and rice meal in the middle of the day, a certain amount of nagging from the teachers, and a few other things, some amazing effects develop. At least, this is what folk say who have had experience.

Now, the Mother Superior of a Convent and the Colonel of a British Infantry Regiment would be justly shocked at any comparison being made between their respective charges. But it is a fact that, under certain circumstances, Thomas in bulk can be worked up into dithering, rippling hysteria. He does not weep, but he shows his trouble unmistakably, and the consequences get into the newspapers, and all the good people who hardly know a Martini from a Snider say: "Take away the brute's ammunition!"

Thomas isn't a brute, and his business, which is to look after the virtuous people, demands that he shall have his ammunition to his hand. He doesn't wear silk stockings, and he really ought to be supplied with a new Adjective to help him to express his opinions: but, for all that, he is a great man. If you call him "the heroic defender of the national honour" one day, and "a brutal and licentious soldiery" the next, you naturally bewilder him, and he looks upon you with suspicion. There is nobody to speak for Thomas except people who have theories to work off on him, and nobody understands Thomas except Thomas, and he does not always know what is the matter with himself.

That is the prologue. This is the story:—

Corporal Slane was engaged to be married to Miss Jhansi M'Kenna, whose history is well known in the regiment and elsewhere. He had his Colonel's permission, and, being popular with the men, every arrangement had been made to give the wedding what Private Ortheris called "eeklar." It fell in the heart of the hot weather, and, after the wedding, Slane was going up to the Hills with the bride. None the less, Slane's grievance was that the affair would be only a hired-carriage wedding, and he felt that the "eeklar" of that was meagre. Miss M'Kenna did not care so much. The Sergeant's wife was helping her to make her wedding-dress, and she was very busy. Slane was, just then, the only moderately contented man in barracks. All the rest were more or less miserable.

And they had so much to make them happy, too. All their work was over at eight in the morning, and for the rest of the day they could lie on their backs and smoke Canteen-plug and swear at the punkah-coolies. They enjoyed a fine, full flesh meal in the middle of the day, and then threw themselves down on their cots and sweated and slept till it was cool enough to go out with their "towny," whose vocabulary contained less than six hundred words, and the Adjective, and whose views on every conceivable question they had heard many times before.

There was the Canteen, of course, and there was the Temperance Room with the second-hand papers in it; but a man of any profession cannot read for eight hours a day in a temperature of 96 deg. or 98 deg. in the shade, running up sometimes to 103 deg. at midnight. Very few men, even though they get a pannikin of flat, stale, muddy beer and hide it under their cots, can continue drinking for six hours a day. One man tried, but he died, and nearly the whole regiment went to his funeral because it gave them something to do. It was too early for the excitement of fever or cholera. The men could only wait and wait and wait, and watch the shadow of the barrack creeping across the blinding white dust. That was a gay life.

They lounged about cantonments—it was too hot for any sort of game, and almost too hot for vice—and fuddled themselves in the evening, and filled themselves to distension with the healthy nitrogenous food provided for them, and the more they stoked the less exercise they took and more explosive they grew. Then tempers began to wear away, and men fell a-brooding over insults real or imaginary, for they had nothing else to think of. The tone of the repartees changed, and instead of saying light-heartedly: "I'll knock your silly face in," men grew laboriously polite and hinted that the cantonments were not big enough for themselves and their enemy, and that there would be more space for one of the two in another Place.

It may have been the Devil who arranged the thing, but the fact of the case is that Losson had for a long time been worrying Simmons in an aimless way. It gave him occupation. The two had their cots side by side, and would sometimes spend a long afternoon swearing at each other; but Simmons was afraid of Losson and dared not challenge him to a fight. He thought over the words in the hot still nights, and half the hate he felt towards Losson he vented on the wretched punkah-coolie.

Losson bought a parrot in the bazar, and put it into a little cage, and lowered the cage into the cool darkness of a well, and sat on the well-curb, shouting bad language down to the parrot. He taught it to say: "Simmons, ye so-oor," which means swine, and several other things entirely unfit for publication. He was a big gross man, and he shook like a jelly when the parrot had the sentence correctly. Simmons, however, shook with rage, for all the room were laughing at him—the parrot was such a disreputable puff of green feathers and it looked so human when it chattered. Losson used to sit, swinging his fat legs, on the side of the cot, and ask the parrot what it thought of Simmons. The parrot would answer: "Simmons, ye so-oor." "Good boy," Losson used to say, scratching the parrot's head; "ye 'ear that, Sim?" And Simmons used to turn over on his stomach and make answer: "I 'ear. Take 'eed you don't 'ear something one of these days."

In the restless nights, after he had been asleep all day, fits of blind rage came upon Simmons and held him till he trembled all over, while he thought in how many different ways he would slay Losson. Sometimes he would picture himself trampling the life out of the man with heavy ammunition-boots, and at others smashing in his face with the butt, and at others jumping on his shoulders and dragging the head back till the neckbone cracked. Then his mouth would feel hot and fevered, and he would reach out for another sup of the beer in the pannikin.

But the fancy that came to him most frequently and stayed with him longest was one connected with the great roll of fat under Losson's right ear. He noticed it first on a moonlight night, and thereafter it was always before his eyes. It was a fascinating roll of fat. A man could get his hand upon it and tear away one side of the neck; or he could place the muzzle of a rifle on it and blow away all the head in a flash. Losson had no right to be sleek and contented and well-to-do, when he, Simmons, was the butt of the room. Some day, perhaps, he would show those who laughed at the "Simmons, ye so-oor" joke, that he was as good as the rest, and held a man's life in the crook of his forefinger. When Losson snored, Simmons hated him more bitterly than ever. Why should Losson be able to sleep when Simmons had to stay awake hour after hour, tossing and turning on the tapes, with the dull liver pain gnawing into his right side and his head throbbing and aching after Canteen? He thought over this for many, many nights, and the world became unprofitable to him. He even blunted his naturally fine appetite with beer and tobacco; and all the while the parrot talked at and made a mock of him.

The heat continued and the tempers wore away more quickly than before. A Sergeant's wife died of heat-apoplexy in the night, and the rumour ran abroad that it was cholera. Men rejoiced openly, hoping that it would spread and send them into camp. But that was a false alarm.

It was late on a Tuesday evening, and the men were waiting in the deep double verandahs for "Last Post," when Simmons went to the box at the foot of his bed, took out his pipe, and slammed the lid down with a bang that echoed through the deserted barrack like the crack of a rifle. Ordinarily speaking, the men would have taken no notice; but their nerves were fretted to fiddle-strings. They jumped up, and three or four clattered into the barrack-room only to find Simmons kneeling by his box.

"Ow! It's you, is it?" they said, and laughed foolishly. "We thought 'twas—"

Simmons rose slowly. If the accident had so shaken his fellows, what would not the reality do?

"You thought it was—did you? And what makes you think?" he said, lashing himself into madness as he went on; "to Hell with your thinking, ye dirty spies!"

"Simmons, ye so-oor," chuckled the parrot in the verandah sleepily, recognising a well-known voice. Now that was absolutely all.

The tension snapped. Simmons fell back on the arm-rack deliberately,— the men were at the far end of the room,—and took out his rifle and packet of ammunition. "Don't go playing the goat, Sim!" said Losson. "Put it down," but there was a quaver in his voice. Another man stooped, slipped his boot, and hurled it at Simmons's head. The prompt answer was a shot which, fired at random, found its billet in Losson's throat. Losson fell forward without a word, and the others scattered.

"You thought it was!" yelled Simmons. "You're drivin' me to it! I tell you you're drivin' me to it! Get up, Losson, an' don't lie shammin' there—you an' your blasted parrit that druv me to it!"

But there was an unaffected reality about Losson's pose that showed Simmons what he had done. The men were still clamouring in the verandah. Simmons appropriated two more packets of ammunition and ran into the moonlight, muttering: "I'll make a night of it. Thirty roun's, an' the last for myself. Take you that, you dogs!"

He dropped on one knee and fired into the brown of the men on the verandah, but the bullet flew high, and landed in the brickwork with a vicious phwit that made some of the younger ones turn pale. It is, as musketry theorists observe, one thing to fire and another to be fired at.

Then the instinct of the chase flared up. The news spread from barrack to barrack, and the men doubled out intent on the capture of Simmons, the wild beast, who was heading for the Cavalry parade-ground, stopping now and again to send back a shot and a curse in the direction of his pursuers.

"I'll learn you to spy on me!" he shouted; "I'll learn you to give me dorg's names! Come on, the 'ole lot o' you! Colonel John Anthony Deever, C. B.!"—he turned towards the Infantry Mess and shook his rifle—"you think yourself the devil of a man—but I tell you that if you put your ugly old carcass outside o' that door, I'll make you the poorest-lookin' man in the army. Come out, Colonel John Anthony Deever, C. B.! Come Out and see me practiss on the rainge. I'm the crack shot of the 'ole bloomin' battalion." In proof of which statement Simmons fired at the lighted windows of the mess-house.

"Private Simmons, E Comp'ny, on the Cavalry p'rade-ground, Sir, with thirty rounds," said a Sergeant breathlessly to the Colonel. "Shootin' right and lef', Sir. Shot Private Losson. What's to be done, Sir?"

Colonel John Anthony Deever, C. B., sallied out, only to be saluted by a spurt of dust at his feet.

"Pull up!" said the Second in Command; "I don't want my step in that way, Colonel. He's as dangerous as a mad dog."

"Shoot him like one, then," said the Colonel bitterly, "if he won't take his chance. My regiment, too! If it had been the Towheads I could have understood."

Private Simmons had occupied a strong position near a well on the edge of the parade-ground, and was defying the regiment to come on. The regiment was not anxious to comply, for there is small honour in being shot by a fellow-private. Only Corporal Slane, rifle in hand, threw himself down on the ground, and wormed his way towards the well.

"Don't shoot," said he to the men round him; "like as not you'll 'it me. I'll catch the beggar livin'."

Simmons ceased shouting for a while, and th noise of trap-wheels could be heard across the plain. Major Oldyne, Commanding the Horse Battery, was coming back from a dinner in the Civil Lines; was driving after his usual custom—that is to say, as fast as the horse could go.

"A orf'cer! A blooming spangled orf'cer!" shrieked Simmons; "I'll make a scarecrow of that orf'cer!" The trap stopped.

"What's this?" demanded the Major of Gunners. "You there, drop your rifle."

"Why, it's Jerry Blazes! I ain't got no quarrel with you, Jerry Blazes. Pass, frien', an' all's well!"

But Jerry Blazes had not the faintest intention of passing a dangerous murderer. He was, as his adoring Battery swore long and fervently, without knowledge of fear, and they were surely the best judges, for Jerry Blazes, it was notorious, had done his possible to kill a man each time the Battery went out.

He walked towards Simmons, with the intention of rushing him and knocking him down.

"Don't make me do it, Sir," said Simmons; "I ain't got nothing ag'in' you. Ah! you would?"—the Major broke into a run—"Take that, then!"

The Major dropped with a bullet through his shoulder, and Simmons stood over him. He had lost the satisfaction of killing Losson in the desired way: but here was a helpless body to his hand. Should he slip in another cartridge, and blow off the head, or with the butt smash in the white face? He stopped to consider, and a cry went up from the far side of the parade-ground: "He's killed Jerry Blazes!" But in the shelter of the well-pillars Simmons was safe, except when he stepped out to fire. "I'll blow yer 'andsome 'ead off, Jerry Blazes," said Simmons reflectively. "Six and three is nine an' one is ten, an' that leaves me another nineteen, an' one for myself." He tugged at the string of the second packet of ammunition. Corporal Slane crawled out of the shadow of a bank into the moonlight.

"I see you!" said Simmons. "Come a bit furder on an' I'll do for you."

"I'm comin'," said Corporal Slane briefly; "you've done a bad day's work, Sim. Come out 'ere an' come back with me."

"Come to," laughed Simmons, sending a cartridge home with his thumb. "Not before I've settled you an' Jerry Blazes."

The Corporal was lying at full length in the dust of the parade-ground, a rifle under him. Some of the less cautious men in the distance shouted: "Shoot 'im! Shoot 'im, Slane!"

"You move 'and or foot, Slane," said Simmons, "an' I'll kick Jerry Blazes' 'ead in, and shoot you after."

"I ain't movin'," said the Corporal, raising his head; "you daren't 'it a man on 'is legs. Let go o' Jerry Blazes an' come out o' that with your fistes. Come an' 'it me. You daren't, you bloomin' dog-shooter!"

"I dare."

"You lie, you man-sticker. You sneakin', Sheeny butcher, you lie. See there!" Slane kicked the rifle away, and stood up in the peril of his life. "Come on, now!"

The temptation was more than Simmons could resist, for the Corporal in his white clothes offered a perfect mark.

"Don't misname me," shouted Simmons, firing as he spoke. The shot missed, and the shooter, blind with rage, threw his rifle down and rushed at Slane from the protection of the well. Within striking distance, he kicked savagely at Slane's stomach, but the weedy Corporal knew something of Simmons's weakness, and knew, too, the deadly guard for that kick. Bowing forward and drawing up his right leg till the heel of the right foot was set some three inches above the inside of the left knee-cap, he met the blow standing on one leg—exactly as Gonds stand when they meditate—and ready for the fall that would follow. There was an oath, the Corporal fell over to his own left as shinbone met shinbone, and the Private collapsed, his right leg broken an inch above the ankle.

"Pity you don't know that guard, Sim," said Slane, spitting out the dust as he rose. Then raising his voice—"Come an' take him on. I've bruk 'is leg." This was not strictly true, for the Private had accomplished his own downfall, since it is the special merit of that leg-guard that the harder the kick the greater the kicker's discomfiture.

Slane walked to Jerry Blazes and hung over him with ostentatious anxiety, while Simmons, weeping with pain, was carried away. "'Ope you ain't 'urt badly, Sir," said Slane. The Major had fainted, and there was an ugly, ragged hole through the top of his arm. Slane knelt down and murmured: "S'elp me, I believe 'e's dead. Well, if that ain't my blooming luck all over!"

But the Major was destined to lead his Battery afield for many a long day with unshaken nerve. He was removed, and nursed and petted into convalescence, while the Battery discussed the wisdom of capturing Simmons and blowing him from a gun. They idolised their Major, and his reappearance on parade brought about a scene nowhere provided for in the Army Regulations.

Great, too, was the glory that fell to Slane's share. The Gunners would have made him drunk thrice a day for at least a fortnight. Even the Colonel of his own regiment complimented him upon his coolness, and the local paper called him a hero. These things did not puff him up. When the Major offered him money and thanks, the virtuous Corporal took the one and put aside the other. But he had a request to make and prefaced it with many a "Beg y' pardon, Sir." Could the Major see his way to letting the Slane-M'Kenna wedding be adorned by the presence of four Battery horses to pull a hired barouche? The Major could, and so could the Battery. Excessively so. It was a gorgeous wedding.

"Wot did I do it for?" said Corporal Slane. "For the 'orses o' course. Jhansi ain't a beauty to look at, but I wasn't goin' to 'ave a hired turnout. Jerry Blazes? If I 'adn't 'a' wanted something, Sim might ha' blowed Jerry Blazes' blooming 'ead into Hirish stew for aught I'd 'a' cared."

And they hanged Private Simmons—hanged him as high as Haman in hollow square of the regiment; and the Colonel said it was Drink; and the Chaplain was sure it was the Devil; and Simmons fancied it was both, but he didn't know, and only hoped his fate would be a warning to his companions; and half a dozen "intelligent publicists" wrote six beautiful leading articles on "The Prevalence of Crime in the Army."

But not a soul thought of comparing the "bloody-minded Simmons" to the squawking, gaping school-girl with which this story opens.

THE LOST LEGION

When the Indian Mutiny broke out, and a little time before the siege of Delhi, a regiment of Native Irregular Horse was stationed at Peshawur on the frontier of India. That regiment caught what John Lawrence called at the time "the prevalent mania," and would have thrown in its lot with the mutineers, had it been allowed to do so. The chance never came, for, as the regiment swept off down south, it was headed off by a remnant of an English corps into the hills of Afghanistan, and there the newly conquered tribesmen turned against it as wolves turn against buck. It was hunted for the sake of its arms and accoutrements from hill to hill, from ravine to ravine, up and down the dried beds of rivers and round the shoulders of bluffs, till it disappeared as water sinks in the sand—this officerless rebel regiment. The only trace left of its existence to-day is a nominal roll drawn up in neat round hand and countersigned by an officer who called himself, "Adjutant, late Irregular Cavalry." The paper is yellow with years and dirt, but on the back of it you can still read a pencil-note by John Lawrence, to this effect: "See that the two native officers who remained loyal are not deprived of their estates.—J. L." Of six hundred and fifty sabres only two stood strain, and John Lawrence in the midst of all the agony of the first months of the Mutiny found time to think about their merits.

That was more than thirty years ago, and the tribesmen across the Afghan border who helped to annihilate the regiment are now old men. Sometimes a graybeard speaks of his share in the massacre. "They came," he will say, "across the border, very proud, calling upon us to rise and kill the English, and go down to the sack of Delhi. But we who had just been conquered by the same English knew that they were over-bold, and that the Government could account easily for those down-country dogs. This Hindustani regiment, therefore, we treated with fair words, and kept standing in one place till the redcoats came after them very hot and angry. Then this regiment ran forward a little more into our hills to avoid the wrath of the English, and we lay upon their flanks watching from the sides of the hills till we were well assured that their path was lost behind them. Then we came down, for we desired their clothes, and their bridles, and their rifles, and their boots—more especially their boots. That was a great killing—done slowly." Here the old man will rub his nose, and shake his long snaky locks, and lick his bearded lips, and grin till the yellow tooth-stumps show. "Yea, we killed them because we needed their gear, and we knew that their lives had been forfeited to God on account of their sin—the sin of treachery to the salt which they had eaten. They rode up and down the valleys, stumbling and rocking in their saddles, and howling for mercy. We drove them slowly like cattle till they were all assembled in one place, the flat wide valley of Sheor Kit. Many had died from want of water, but there still were many left, and they could not make any stand. We went among them pulling them down with our hands two at a time, and our boys killed them who were new to the sword. My share of the plunder was such and such—so many guns, and so many saddles. The guns were good in those days. Now we steal the Government rifles, and despise smooth barrels. Yes, beyond doubt we wiped that regiment from off the face of the earth, and even the memory of the deed is now dying. But men say—"

At this point the tale would stop abruptly, and it was impossible to find out what men said across the border. The Afghans were always a secretive race, and vastly preferred doing something wicked to saying anything at all. They would be quiet and well-behaved for months, till one night, without word or warning, they would rush a police-post, cut the throats of a constable or two, dash through a village, carry away three or four women, and withdraw, in the red glare of burning thatch, driving the cattle and goats before them to their own desolate hills. The Indian Government would become almost tearful on these occasions. First it would say, "Please be good and we'll forgive you." The tribe concerned in the latest depredation would collectively put its thumb to its nose and answer rudely. Then the Government would say: "Hadn't you better pay up a little money for those few corpses you left behind you the other night?" Here the tribe would temporise, and lie and bully, and some of the younger men, merely to show contempt of authority, would raid another police-post and fire into some frontier mud-fort, and, if lucky, kill a real English officer. Then the Government would say:—

"Observe; if you really persist in this line of conduct, you will be hurt." If the tribe knew exactly what was going on in India, it would apologise or be rude, according as it learned whether the Government was busy with other things or able to devote its full attention to their performances. Some of the tribes knew to one corpse how far to go. Others became excited, lost their heads, and told the Government to come on. With sorrow and tears, and one eye on the British taxpayer at home, who insisted on regarding these exercises as brutal wars of annexation, the Government would prepare an expensive little field-brigade and some guns, and send all up into the hills to chase the wicked tribe out of the valleys, where the corn grew, into the hill-tops, where there was nothing to eat. The tribe would turn out in full strength and enjoy the campaign, for they knew that their women would never be touched, that their wounded would be nursed, not mutilated, and that as soon as each man's bag of corn was spent they could surrender and palaver with the English General as though they had been a real enemy. Afterwards, years afterwards, they would pay the blood-money, driblet by driblet, to the Government, and tell their children how they had slain the redcoats by thousands. The only drawback to this kind of picnic-war was the weakness of the redcoats for solemnly blowing up with powder their fortified towers and keeps. This the tribes always considered mean.

Chief among the leaders of the smaller tribes—the little clans who knew to a penny the expense of moving white troops against them—was a priest-bandit-chief whom we will call the Gulla Kutta Mullah. His enthusiasm for Border murder as an art was almost dignified. He would cut down a mail-runner from pure wantonness, or bombard a mud-fort with rifle-fire when he knew that our men needed to sleep. In his leisure moments he would go on circuit among his neighbours, and try to incite other tribes to devilry. Also, he kept a kind of hotel for fellow-outlaws in his own village, which lay in a valley called Bersund. Any respectable murderer on that section of the frontier was sure to lie up at Bersund, for it was reckoned an exceedingly safe place. The sole entry to it ran through a narrow gorge which could be converted into a death-trap in five minutes. It was surrounded by high hills, reckoned inaccessible to all save born mountaineers, and here the Gulla Kutta Mullah lived in great state, the head of a colony of mud and stone huts, and in each mud hut hung some portion of a red uniform and the plunder of dead men. The Government particularly wished for his capture, and once invited him formally to come out and be hanged on account of the many murders in which he had taken a direct part. He replied:—

"I am only twenty miles, as the crow flies, from your border. Come and fetch me."

"Some day we will come," said the Government, "and hanged you will be."

The Gulla Kutta Mullah let the matter slip from his mind. He knew that the patience of the Government was as long as a summer day; but he did not realise that its arm was as long as a winter night. Months afterwards, when there was peace on the border, and all India was quiet, the Indian Government turned in its sleep and remembered the Gulla Kutta Mullah at Bersund, with his thirteen outlaws. The movement against him of one single regiment—which the telegrams would have translated as war—would have been highly impolitic. This was a time for silence and speed, and, above all, absence of bloodshed.

You must know that all along the north-west frontier of India there is spread a force of some thirty thousand foot and horse, whose duty it is to quietly and unostentatiously shepherd the tribes in front of them. They move up and down, and down and up, from one desolate little post to another; they are ready to take the field at ten minutes' notice; they are always half in and half out of a difficulty somewhere along the monotonous line; their lives are as hard as their own muscles, and the papers never say anything about them. It was from this force that the Government picked its men.

One night, at a station where the mounted Night Patrol fire as they challenge, and the wheat rolls in great blue-green waves under our cold northern moon, the officers were playing billiards in the mud-walled club-house, when orders came to them that they were to go on parade at once for a night-drill. They grumbled, and went to turn out their men—a hundred English troops, let us say, two hundred Goorkhas, and about a hundred cavalry of the finest native cavalry in the world.

When they were on the parade-ground, it was explained to them in whispers that they must set off at once across the hills to Bersund. The English troops were to post themselves round the hills at the side of the valley; the Goorkhas would command the gorge and the death-trap, and the cavalry would fetch a long march round and get to the back of the circle of hills, whence, if there were any difficulty, they could charge down on the Mullah's men. But orders were very strict that there should be no fighting and no noise. They were to return in the morning with every round of ammunition intact, and the Mullah and the thirteen outlaws bound in their midst. If they were successful, no one would know or care anything about their work; but failure meant probably a small border war, in which the Gulla Kutta Mullah would pose as a popular leader against a big bullying power, instead of a common Border murderer.

Then there was silence, broken only by the clicking of the compass-needles and snapping of watch-cases, as the heads of columns compared bearings and made appointments for the rendezvous. Five minutes later the parade-ground was empty; the green coats of the Goorkhas and the overcoats of the English troops had faded into the darkness, and the cavalry were cantering away in the face of a blinding drizzle.

What the Goorkhas and the English did will be seen later on. The heavy work lay with the horses, for they had to go far and pick their way clear of habitations. Many of the troopers were natives of that part of the world, ready and anxious to fight against their kin, and some of the officers had made private and unofficial excursions into those hills before. They crossed the border, found a dried river-bed, cantered up that, walked through a stony gorge, risked crossing a low hill under cover of the darkness, skirted another hill, leaving their hoof-marks deep in some ploughed ground, felt their way along another water-course, ran over the neck of a spur praying that no one would hear their horses grunting, and so worked on in the rain and the darkness till they had left Bersund and its crater of hills a little behind them, and to the left, and it was time to swing round. The ascent commanding the back of Bersund was steep, and they halted to draw breath in a broad level valley below the height. That is to say, the men reined up, but the horses, blown as they were, refused to halt. There was unchristian language, the worse for being delivered in a whisper, and you heard the saddles squeaking in the darkness as the horses plunged.

The subaltern at the rear of one troop turned in his saddle and said very softly:—

"Carter, what the blessed heavens are you doing at the rear? Bring your men up, man."

There was no answer, till a trooper replied:—

"Carter Sahib is forward—not here. There is nothing behind us."

"There is," said the subaltern. "The squadron's walking on its own tail."

Then the Major in command moved down to the rear, swearing softly and asking for the blood of Lieutenant Halley—the subaltern who had just spoken.

"Look after your rearguard," said the Major. "Some of your infernal thieves have got lost. They're at the head of the squadron, and you're a several kinds of idiot."

"Shall I tell off my men, sir?" said the subaltern sulkily, for he was feeling wet and cold.

"Tell 'em off!" said the Major. "Whip 'em off, by Gad! You're squandering them all over the place. There's a troop behind you now!"

"So I was thinking," said the subaltern calmly. "I have all my men here, sir. Better speak to Carter."

"Carter Sahib sends salaam and wants to know why the regiment is stopping," said a trooper to Lieutenant Halley.

"Where under heaven is Carter," said the Major.

"Forward with his troop," was the answer.

"Are we walking in a ring, then, or are we the centre of a blessed brigade?" said the Major.

By this time there was silence all along the column. The horses were still; but, through the drive of the fine rain, men could hear the feet of many horses moving over stony ground.

"We're being stalked," said Lieutenant Halley.

"They've no horses here. Besides they'd have fired before this," said the Major. "It's—it's villagers' ponies."

"Then our horses would have neighed and spoilt the attack long ago. They must have been near us for half an hour," said the subaltern.

"Queer that we can't smell the horses," said the Major, damping his finger and rubbing it on his nose as he sniffed up wind.

"Well, it's a bad start," said the subaltern, shaking the wet from his overcoat. "What shall we do, sir?"

"Get on," said the Major. "We shall catch it to-night."

The column moved forward very gingerly for a few paces. Then there was an oath, a shower of blue sparks as shod hooves crashed on small stones, and a man rolled over with a jangle of accoutrements that would have waked the dead.

"Now we've gone and done it," said Lieutenant Halley. "All the hillside awake and all the hillside to climb in the face of musketry-fire! This comes of trying to do night-hawk work."

The trembling trooper picked himself up and tried to explain that his horse had fallen over one of the little cairns that are built of loose stones on the spot where a man has been murdered. There was no need to give reasons. The Major's big Australian charger blundered next, and the column came to a halt in what seemed to be a very graveyard of little cairns, all about two feet high. The manoeuvres of the squadron are not reported. Men said that it felt like mounted quadrilles without training and without the music; but at last the horses, breaking rank and choosing their own way, walked clear of the cairns, till every man of the squadron reformed and drew rein a few yards up the slope of the hill. Then, according to Lieutenant Halley, there was another scene very like the one which has been described. The Major and Carter insisted that all the men had not joined rank, and that there were more of them in the rear, clicking and blundering among the dead men's cairns. Lieutenant Halley told off his own troopers again and resigned himself to wait. Later on he said to me:

"I didn't much know and I didn't much care what was going on. The row of that trooper falling ought to have scared half the country, and I would take my oath that we were being stalked by a full regiment in the rear, and they were making row enough to rouse all Afghanistan. I sat tight, but nothing happened."

The mysterious part of the night's work was the silence on the hillside. Everybody knew that the Gulla Kutta Mullah had his outpost-huts on the reverse side of the hill, and everybody expected, by the time that the Major had sworn himself into quiet, that the watchmen there would open fire. When nothing happened, they said that the gusts of the rain had deadened the sound of the horses, and thanked Providence. At last the Major satisfied himself (a) that he had left no one behind among the cairns, and (b) that he was not being taken in the rear by a large and powerful body of cavalry. The men's tempers were thoroughly spoiled, the horses were lathered and unquiet, and one and all prayed for the daylight.

They set themselves to climb up the hill, each man leading his mount carefully. Before they had covered the lower slopes or the breast-plates had begun to tighten, a thunderstorm came up behind, rolling across the low hills and drowning any noise less than that of cannon. The first flash of the lightning showed the bare ribs of the ascent, the hill-crest standing steely-blue against the black sky, the little falling lines of the rain, and, a few yards to their left flank, an Afghan watch-tower, two-storied, built of stone, and entered by a ladder from the upper story. The ladder was up, and a man with a rifle was leaning from the window. The darkness and the thunder rolled down in an instant, and, when the lull followed, a voice from the watch-tower cried, "Who goes there?"

The cavalry were very quiet, but each man gripped his carbine and stood beside his horse. Again the voice called, "Who goes there?" and in a louder key, "O brothers, give the alarm!" Now, every man in the cavalry would have died in his long boots sooner than have asked for quarter, but it is a fact that the answer to the second call was a long wail of "Marf karo! Marf karo!" which means, "Have mercy! Have mercy!" It came from the climbing regiment.

The cavalry stood dumbfoundered, till the big troopers had time to whisper one to another: "Mir Khan, was that thy voice? Abdullah, didst thou call?" Lieutenant Halley stood beside his charger and waited. So long as no firing was going on he was content. Another flash of lightning showed the horses with heaving flanks and nodding heads; the men, white eye-balled, glaring beside them, and the stone watch-tower to the left. This time there was no head at the window, and the rude iron-clamped shutter that could turn a rifle-bullet was closed.

"Go on, men," said the Major. "Get up to the top at any rate!" The squadron toiled forward, the horses wagging their tails and the men pulling at the bridles, the stones rolling down the hillside and the sparks flying. Lieutenant Halley declares that he never heard a squadron make so much noise in his life. They scrambled up, he said, as though each horse had eight legs and a spare horse to follow him. Even then there was no sound from the watch-tower, and the men stopped exhausted on the ridge that overlooked the pit of darkness in which the village of Bersund lay. Girths were loosed, curb-chains shifted, and saddles adjusted, and the men dropped down among the stones. Whatever might happen now, they held the upper ground of any attack.

The thunder ceased, and with it the rain, and the soft thick darkness of a winter night before the dawn covered them all. Except for the sound of falling water among the ravines below, everything was still. They heard the shutter of the watch-tower below them thrown back with a clang, and the voice of the watcher calling, "Oh, Hafiz Ullah!"

The echoes took up the call, "La-la-la!" and an answer came from the watch-tower hidden round the curve of the hill, "What is it, Shahbaz Khan?"

Shahbaz Khan replied in the high-pitched voice of the mountaineer: "Hast thou seen?"

The answer came back: "Yes. God deliver us from all evil spirits!"

There was a pause, and then: "Hafiz Ullah, I am alone! Come to me."

"Shahbaz Khan, I am alone also; but I dare not leave my post!"

"That is a lie; thou art afraid."

A longer pause followed, and then: "I am afraid. Be silent! They are below us still. Pray to God and sleep."

The troopers listened and wondered, for they could not understand what save earth and stone could lie below the watch-towers.

Shahbaz Khan began to call again: "They are below us. I can see them! For the pity of God come over to me, Hafiz Ullah! My father slew ten of them. Come over!"

Hafiz Ullah answered in a very loud voice, "Mine was guiltless. Hear, ye Men of the Night, neither my father nor my blood had any part in that sin. Bear thou thine own punishment, Shahbaz Khan."

"Oh, some one ought to stop those two chaps crowing away like cocks there," said the Lieutenant, shivering under his rock.

He had hardly turned round to expose a new side of him to the rain before a bearded, long-locked, evil-smelling Afghan rushed up the hill, and tumbled into his arms. Halley sat upon him, and thrust as much of a sword-hilt as could be spared down the man's gullet. "If you cry out, I kill you," he said cheerfully.

The man was beyond any expression of terror. He lay and quaked, gasping. When Halley took the sword-hilt from between his teeth, he was still inarticulate, but clung to Halley's arm, feeling it from elbow to wrist.

"The Rissala! The dead Rissala!" he gasped, "It is down there!"

"No; the Rissala, the very much alive Rissala. It is up here," said Halley, unshipping his watering-bridle and fastening the man's hands. "Why were you in the towers so foolish as to let us pass?"

"The valley is full of the dead," said the Afghan. "It is better to fall into the hands of the English than the hands of the dead. They march to and fro below there. I saw them in the lightning."

He recovered his composure after a little, and whispering, because Halley's pistol was at his stomach, said: "What is this? There is no war between us now, and the Mullah will kill me for not seeing you pass!"

"Rest easy," said Halley; "we are coming to kill the Mullah, if God please. His teeth have grown too long. No harm will come to thee unless the daylight shows thee as a face which is desired by the gallows for crime done. But what of the dead regiment?"

"I only kill within my own border," said the man, immensely relieved. "The dead regiment is below. The men must have passed through it on their journey—four hundred dead on horses, stumbling among their own graves, among the little heaps—dead men all, whom we slew."

"Whew!" said Halley. "That accounts for my cursing Carter and the Major cursing me. Four hundred sabres, eh? No wonder we thought there were a few extra men in the troop. Kurruk Shah," he whispered to a grizzled native officer that lay within a few feet of him, "hast thou heard anything of a dead Rissala in these hills?

"Assuredly," said Kurruk Shah with a grim chuckle. "Otherwise, why did I, who have served the Queen for seven-and-twenty years, and killed many hill-dogs, shout aloud for quarter when the lightning revealed us to the watch-towers? When I was a young man I saw the killing in the valley of Sheor-Kit there at our feet, and I know the tale that grew up therefrom. But how can the ghosts of unbelievers prevail against us who are of the Faith? Strap that dog's hands a little tighter, Sahib. An Afghan is like an eel."

"But a dead Rissala," said Halley, jerking his captive's wrist. "That is foolish talk, Kurruk Shah. The dead are dead. Hold still, Sag." The Afghan wriggled.

"The dead are dead, and for that reason they walk at night. What need to talk? We be men; we have our eyes and ears. Thou canst both see and hear them down the hillside," said Kurruk Shah composedly.

Halley stared and listened long and intently. The valley was full of stifled noises, as every valley must be at night; but whether he saw or heard more than was natural Halley alone knows, and he does not choose to speak on the subject.

At last, and just before the dawn, a green rocket shot up from the far side of the valley of Bersund, at the head of the gorge, to show that the Goorkhas were in position. A red light from the infantry at left and right answered it, and the cavalry burnt a white flare. Afghans in winter are late sleepers, and it was not till full day that the Gulla Kutta Mullah's men began to straggle from their huts, rubbing their eyes. They saw men in green, and red, and brown uniforms, leaning on their arms, neatly arranged all round the crater of the village of Bersund, in a cordon that not even a wolf could have broken. They rubbed their eyes the more when a pink-faced young man, who was not even in the Army, but represented the Political Department, tripped down the hillside with two orderlies, rapped at the door of the Gulla Kutta Mullah's house, and told him quietly to step out and be tied up for safe transport. That same young man passed on through the huts, tapping here one cateran and there another lightly with his cane; and as each was pointed out, so he was tied up, staring hopelessly at the crowned heights around where the English soldiers looked down with incurious eyes. Only the Mullah tried to carry it off with curses and high words, till a soldier who was tying his hands said:—

"None o' your lip! Why didn't you come out when you was ordered, instead o' keeping us awake all night? You're no better than my own barrack-sweeper, you white-'eaded old polyanthus! Kim up!"

Half an hour later the troops had gone away with the Mullah and his thirteen friends. The dazed villagers were looking ruefully at a pile of broken muskets and snapped swords, and wondering how in the world they had come so to miscalculate the forbearance of the Indian Government.

It was a very neat little affair, neatly carried out, and the men concerned were unofficially thanked for their services.

Yet it seems to me that much credit is also due to another regiment whose name did not appear in brigade orders, and whose very existence is in danger of being forgotten.

THE DRUMS OF THE FORE AND AFT

In the Army List they still stand as "The Fore and Fit Princess Hohenzollern-Sigmaringen-Anspach's Merther-Tydfilshire Own Royal Loyal Light Infantry, Regimental District 329A," but the Army through all its barracks and canteens knows them now as the "Fore and Aft." They may in time do something that shall make their new title honourable, but at present they are bitterly ashamed, and the man who calls them "Fore and Aft" does so at the risk of the head which is on his shoulders.

Two words breathed into the stables of a certain Cavalry Regiment will bring the men out into the streets with belts and mops and bad language; but a whisper of "Fore and Aft" will bring out this regiment with rifles.

Their one excuse is that they came again and did their best to finish the job in style. But for a time all their world knows that they were openly beaten, whipped, dumb-cowed, shaking and afraid. The men know it; their officers know it; the Horse Guards know it, and when the next war comes the enemy will know it also. There are two or three regiments of the Line that have a black mark against their names which they will then wipe out; and it will be excessively inconvenient for the troops upon whom they do their wiping.

The courage of the British soldier is officially supposed to be above proof, and, as a general rule, it is so. The exceptions are decently shovelled out of sight, only to be referred to in the freshest of unguarded talk that occasionally swamps a Mess-table at midnight. Then one hears strange and horrible stories of men not following their officers, of orders being given by those who had no right to give them, and of disgrace that, but for the standing luck of the British Army, might have ended in brilliant disaster. These are unpleasant stories to listen to, and the Messes tell them under their breath, sitting by the big wood fires, and the young officer bows his head and thinks to himself, please God, his men shall never behave unhandily.

The British soldier is not altogether to be blamed for occasional lapses; but this verdict he should not know. A moderately intelligent General will waste six months in mastering the craft of the particular war that he may be waging; a Colonel may utterly misunderstand the capacity of his regiment for three months after it has taken the field, and even a Company Commander may err and be deceived as to the temper and temperament of his own handful: wherefore the soldier, and the soldier of to-day more particularly, should not be blamed for falling back. He should be shot or hanged afterwards—to encourage the others; but he should not be vilified in newspapers, for that is want of tact and waste of space.

He has, let us say, been in the service of the Empress for, perhaps, four years. He will leave in another two years. He has no inherited morals, and four years are not sufficient to drive toughness into his fibre, or to teach him how holy a thing is his Regiment. He wants to drink, he wants to enjoy himself—in India he wants to save money—and he does not in the least like getting hurt. He has received just sufficient education to make him understand half the purport of the orders he receives, and to speculate on the nature of clean, incised, and shattering wounds. Thus, if he is told to deploy under fire preparatory to an attack, he knows that he runs a very great risk of being killed while he is deploying, and suspects that he is being thrown away to gain ten minutes' time. He may either deploy with desperate swiftness, or he may shuffle, or bunch, or break, according to the discipline under which he has lain for four years.

Armed with imperfect knowledge, cursed with the rudiments of an imagination, hampered by the intense selfishness of the lower classes, and unsupported by any regimental associations, this young man is suddenly introduced to an enemy who in eastern lands is always ugly, generally tall and hairy, and frequently noisy. If he looks to the right and the left and sees old soldiers—men of twelve years' service, who, he knows, know what they are about—taking a charge, rush, or demonstration without embarrassment, he is consoled and applies his shoulder to the butt of his rifle with a stout heart. His peace is the greater if he hears a senior, who has taught him his soldiering and broken his head on occasion, whispering: "They'll shout and carry on like this for five minutes. Then they'll rush in, and then we've got 'em by the short hairs!"

But, on the other hand, if he sees only men of his own term of service, turning white and playing with their triggers and saying: "What the Hell's up now?" while the Company Commanders are sweating into their sword-hilts and shouting: "Front rank, fix bayonets. Steady there—steady! Sight for three hundred—no, for five! Lie down, all! Steady! Front rank kneel!" and so forth, he becomes unhappy, and grows acutely miserable when he hears a comrade turn over with the rattle of fire-irons falling into the fender, and the grunt of a pole-axed ox. If he can be moved about a little and allowed to watch the effect of his own fire on the enemy he feels merrier, and may be then worked up to the blind passion of fighting, which is, contrary to general belief, controlled by a chilly Devil and shakes men like ague. If he is not moved about, and begins to feel cold at the pit of the stomach, and in that crisis is badly mauled and hears orders that were never given, he will break, and he will break badly, and of all things under the light of the Sun there is nothing more terrible than a broken British regiment. When the worst comes to the worst and the panic is really epidemic, the men must be e'en let go, and the Company Commanders had better escape to the enemy and stay there for safety's sake. If they can be made to come again they are not pleasant men to meet; because they will not break twice.

About thirty years from this date, when we have succeeded in half-educating everything that wears trousers, our Army will be a beautifully unreliable machine. It will know too much and it will do too little. Later still, when all men are at the mental level of the officer of to-day, it will sweep the earth. Speaking roughly, you must employ either blackguards or gentlemen, or, best of all, blackguards commanded by gentlemen, to do butcher's work with efficiency and despatch. The ideal soldier should, of course, think for himself—the "Pocket-book" says so. Unfortunately, to attain this virtue, he has to pass through the phase of thinking of himself, and that is misdirected genius. A blackguard may be slow to think for himself, but he is genuinely anxious to kill, and a little punishment teaches him how to guard his own skin and perforate another's. A powerfully prayerful Highland Regiment, officered by rank Presbyterians, is, perhaps, one degree more terrible in action than a hard-bitten thousand of irresponsible Irish ruffians led by most improper young unbelievers. But these things prove the rule—which is that the midway men are not to be trusted alone. They have ideas about the value of life and an upbringing that has not taught them to go on and take the chances. They are carefully unprovided with a backing of comrades who have been shot over, and until that backing is re-introduced, as a great many Regimental Commanders intend it shall be, they are more liable to disgrace themselves than the size of the Empire or the dignity of the Army allows. Their officers are as good as good can be, because their training begins early, and God has arranged that a clean-run youth of the British middle classes shall, in the matter of backbone, brains, and bowels, surpass all other youths. For this reason a child of eighteen will stand up, doing nothing, with a tin sword in his hand and joy in his heart until he is dropped. If he dies, he dies like a gentleman. If he lives, he writes Home that he has been "potted," "sniped," "chipped," or "cut over," and sits down to besiege Government for a wound-gratuity until the next little war breaks out, when he perjures himself before a Medical Board, blarneys his Colonel, burns incense round his Adjutant, and is allowed to go to the Front once more.

Which homily brings me directly to a brace of the most finished little fiends that ever banged drum or tootled fife in the Band of a British Regiment. They ended their sinful career by open and flagrant mutiny and were shot for it. Their names were Jakin and Lew—Piggy Lew and they were bold, bad drummer-boys, both of them frequently birched by the Drum-Major of the Fore and Aft.

Jakin was a stunted child of fourteen, and Lew was about the same age. When not looked after, they smoked and drank. They swore habitually after the manner of the Barrack-room, which is cold swearing and comes from between clenched teeth, and they fought religiously once a week. Jakin had sprung from some London gutter, and may or may not have passed through Dr. Barnardo's hands ere he arrived at the dignity of drummer-boy. Lew could remember nothing except the Regiment and the delight of listening to the Band from his earliest years. He hid somewhere in his grimy little soul a genuine love for music, and was most mistakenly furnished with the head of a cherub: insomuch that beautiful ladies who watched the Regiment in church were wont to speak of him as a "darling." They never heard his vitriolic comments on their manners and morals, as he walked back to barracks with the Band and matured fresh causes of offence against Jakin.

The other drummer-boys hated both lads on account of their illogical conduct. Jakin might be pounding Lew, or Lew might be rubbing Jakin's head in the dirt, but any attempt at aggression on the part of an outsider was met by the combined forces of Lew and Jakin; and the consequences were painful. The boys were the Ishmaels of the corps, but wealthy Ishmaels, for they sold battles in alternate weeks for the sport of the barracks when they were not pitted against other boys; and thus amassed money.

On this particular day there was dissension in the camp. They had just been convicted afresh of smoking, which is bad for little boys who use plug-tobacco, and Lew's contention was that Jakin had "stunk so 'orrid bad from keepin' the pipe in pocket," that he and he alone was responsible for the birching they were both tingling under.

"I tell you I 'id the pipe back o' barracks," said Jakin pacifically.

"You're a bloomin' liar," said Lew without heat.

"You're a bloomin' little barstard," said Jakin, strong in the knowledge that his own ancestry was unknown.

Now there is one word in the extended vocabulary of barrack-room abuse that cannot pass without comment. You may call a man a thief and risk nothing. You may even call him a coward without finding more than a boot whiz past your ear, but you must not call a man a bastard unless you are prepared to prove it on his front teeth.

"You might ha' kep' that till I wasn't so sore," said Lew sorrowfully, dodging round Jakin's guard.

"I'll make you sorer," said Jakin genially, and got home on Lew's alabaster forehead. All would have gone well and this story, as the books say, would never have been written, had not his evil fate prompted the Bazar-Sergeant's son, a long, employless man of five-and-twenty, to put in an appearance after the first round. He was eternally in need of money, and knew that the boys had silver.

"Fighting again," said he. "I'll report you to my father, and he'll report you to the Colour-Sergeant."

"What's that to you?" said Jakin with an unpleasant dilation of the nostrils.

"Oh! nothing to me. You'll get into trouble, and you've been up too often to afford that."

"What the Hell do you know about what we've done?" asked Lew the Seraph. "You aren't in the Army, you lousy, cadging civilian."

He closed in on the man's left flank.

"Jes' 'cause you find two gentlemen settlin' their diff'rences with their fistes you stick in your ugly nose where you aren't wanted. Run 'ome to your 'arf-caste slut of a Ma—or we'll give you what-for," said Jakin.

The man attempted reprisals by knocking the boys' heads together. The scheme would have succeeded had not Jakin punched him vehemently in the stomach, or had Lew refrained from kicking his shins. They fought together, bleeding and breathless, for half an hour, and, after heavy punishment, triumphantly pulled down their opponent as terriers pull down a jackal.

"Now," gasped Jakin, "I'll give you what-for." He proceeded to pound the man's features while Lew stamped on the outlying portions of his anatomy. Chivalry is not a strong point in the composition of the average drummer-boy. He fights, as do his betters, to make his mark.

Ghastly was the ruin that escaped, and awful was the wrath of the Bazar-Sergeant. Awful too was the scene in Orderly-room when the two reprobates appeared to answer the charge of half-murdering a "civilian." The Bazar-Sergeant thirsted for a criminal action, and his son lied. The boys stood to attention while the black clouds of evidence accumulated.

"You little devils are more trouble than the rest of the Regiment put together," said the Colonel angrily. "One might as well admonish thistledown, and I can't well put you in cells or under stoppages. You must be birched again."

"Beg y' pardon, Sir. Can't we say nothin' in our own defence, Sir?" shrilled Jakin.

"Hey! What? Are you going to argue with me?" said the Colonel.

"No, Sir," said Lew. "But if a man come to you, Sir, and said he was going to report you, Sir, for 'aving a bit of a turn-up with a friend, Sir, an' wanted to get money out o' you, Sir-"

The Orderly-room exploded in a roar of laughter. "Well?" said the Colonel.

"That was what that measly jarnwar there did, Sir, and 'e'd 'a' done it, Sir, if we 'adn't prevented 'im. We didn't 'it 'im much, Sir. 'E 'adn't no manner o' right to interfere with us, Sir. I don't mind bein' birched by the Drum-Major, Sir, nor yet reported by any Corp'ral, but I'm—but I don't think it's fair, Sir, for a civilian to come an' talk over a man in the Army."

A second shout of laughter shook the Orderly-room, but the Colonel was grave.

"What sort of characters have these boys?" he asked of the Regimental Sergeant-Major.

"Accordin' to the Bandmaster, Sir," returned that revered official—the only soul in the Regiment whom the boys feared—"they do everything but lie, Sir."

"Is it like we'd go for that man for fun, Sir?" said Lew, pointing to the plaintiff.

"Oh, admonished—admonished!" said the Colonel testily, and when the boys had gone he read the Bazar-Sergeant's son a lecture on the sin of unprofitable meddling, and gave orders that the Bandmaster should keep the Drums in better discipline.

"If either of you come to practice again with so much as a scratch on your two ugly little faces," thundered the Bandmaster, "I'll tell the Drum-Major to take the skin off your backs. Understand that, you young devils."

Then he repented of his speech for just the length of time that Lew, looking like a seraph in red worsted embellishments, took the place of one of the trumpets—in hospital—and rendered the echo of a battle-piece. Lew certainly was a musician, and had often in his more exalted moments expressed a yearning to master every instrument of the Band.

"There's nothing to prevent your becoming a Bandmaster, Lew," said the Bandmaster, who had composed waltzes of his own, and worked day and night in the interests of the Band.

"What did he say?" demanded Jakin after practice.

"Said I might be a bloomin' Bandmaster, an' be asked in to 'ave a glass o' sherry wine on Mess-nights."

"Ho! 'Said you might be a bloomin' noncombatant, did 'e! That's just about wot 'e would say. When I've put in my boy's service it's a bloomin' shame that doesn't count for pension—I'll take on as a privit. Then I'll be a Lance in a year—knowin' what I know about the ins an' outs o' things. In three years I'll be a bloomin' Sergeant. I won't marry then, not I! I'll 'old on and learn the orf'cers' ways an' apply for exchange into a reg'ment that doesn't know all about me. Then I'll be a bloomin' orf'cer. Then I'll ask you to 'ave a glass o' sherry wine, Mister Lew, an' you'll bloomin' well 'ave to stay in the hanty-room while the Mess-Sergeant brings it to your dirty 'ands."

"S'pose I'm going to be a Bandmaster? Not I, quite. I'll be a orf'cer too. There's nothin' like takin' to a thing an' stickin' to it, the Schoolmaster says. The Reg'ment don't go 'ome for another seven years. I'll be a Lance then or near to."

Thus the boys discussed their futures, and conducted themselves piously for a week. That is to say, Lew started a flirtation with the Colour-Sergeant's daughter, aged thirteen—"not," as he explained to Jakin, "with any intention o' matrimony, but by way o' keep in' my 'and in." And the black-haired Cris Delighan enjoyed that flirtation more than previous ones, and the other drummer-boys raged furiously together, and Jakin preached sermons on the dangers of bein' tangled along o' petticoats.

But neither love nor virtue would have held Lew long in the paths of propriety had not the rumour gone abroad that the Regiment was to be sent on active service, to take part in a war which, for the sake of brevity, we will call "The War of the Lost Tribes."

The barracks had the rumour almost before the Mess-room, and of all the nine hundred men in barracks, not ten had seen a shot fired in anger. The Colonel had, twenty years ago, assisted at a Frontier expedition; one of the Majors had seen service at the Cape; a confirmed deserter in E Company had helped to clear streets in Ireland; but that was all. The Regiment had been put by for many years. The overwhelming mass of its rank and file had from three to four years' service; the non-commissioned officers were under thirty years old; and men and sergeants alike had forgotten to speak of the stories written in brief upon the Colours—the New Colours that had been formally blessed by an Archbishop in England ere the Regiment came away. They wanted to go to the Front—they were enthusiastically anxious to go—but they had no knowledge of what war meant, and there was none to tell them. They were an educated regiment, the percentage of school-certificates in their ranks was high, and most of the men could do more than read and write. They had been recruited in loyal observance of the territorial idea; but they themselves had no notion of that idea. They were made up of drafts from an over-populated manufacturing district. The system had put flesh and muscle upon their small bones, but it could not put heart into the sons of those who for generations had done overmuch work for overscanty pay, had sweated in drying-rooms, stooped over looms, coughed among white-lead, and shivered on lime-barges. The men had found food and rest in the Army, and now they were going to fight "niggers"—people who ran away if you shook a stick at them. Wherefore they cheered lustily when the rumour ran, and the shrewd, clerkly non-commissioned officers speculated on the chances of batta and of saving their pay. At Headquarters men said: "The Fore and Fit have never been under fire within the last generation. Let us, therefore, break them in easily by setting them to guard lines of communication." And this would have been done but for the fact that British Regiments were wanted—badly wanted—at the Front, and there were doubtful Native Regiments that could fill the minor duties. "Brigade 'em with two strong Regiments," said Headquarters. "They may be knocked about a bit, but they'll learn their business before they come through. Nothing like a night-alarm and a little cutting-up of stragglers to make a Regiment smart in the field. Wait till they've had half a dozen sentries' throats cut."

The Colonel wrote with delight that the temper of his men was excellent, that the Regiment was all that could be wished, and as sound as a bell. The Majors smiled with a sober joy, and the subalterns waltzed in pairs down the Mess-room after dinner, and nearly shot themselves at revolver-practice. But there was consternation in the hearts of Jakin and Lew. What was to be done with the Drums? Would the Band go to the Front? How many of the Drums would accompany the Regiment?

They took counsel together, sitting in a tree and smoking.

"It's more than a bloomin' toss-up they'll leave us be'ind at the Depot with the women. You'll like that," said Jakin sarcastically.

"Cause o' Cris, y' mean? Wot's a woman, or a 'ole bloomin' depot o' women, 'longside o' the chanst of field-service? You know I'm as keen on goin' as you," said Lew.

"Wish I was a bloomin' bugler," said Jakin sadly. "They'll take Tom Kidd along, that I can plaster a wall with, an' like as not they won't take us."

"Then let's go an' make Tom Kidd so bloomin' sick 'e can't bugle no more. You 'old 'is 'ands an' I'll kick him," said Lew, wriggling on the branch.

"That ain't no good neither. We ain't the sort o' characters to presoom on our rep'tations—they're bad. If they have the Band at the Depot we don't go, and no error there. If they take the Band we may get cast for medical unfitness. Are you medical fit, Piggy?" said Jakin, digging Lew in the ribs with force.

"Yus," said Lew with an oath. "The Doctor says your 'eart's weak through smokin' on an empty stummick. Throw a chest an' I'll try yer."

Jakin threw out his chest, which Lew smote with all his might. Jakin turned very pale, gasped, crowed, screwed up his eyes, and said—"That's all right."

"You'll do," said Lew. "I've 'eard o' men dying when you 'it 'em fair on the breastbone."

"Don't bring us no nearer goin', though," said Jakin. "Do you know where we're ordered?"

"Gawd knows, an' 'E won't split on a pal. Somewheres up to the Front to kill Paythans—hairy big beggars that turn you inside out if they get 'old o' you. They say their women are good-looking, too."

"Any loot?" asked the abandoned Jakin.

"Not a bloomin' anna, they say, unless you dig up the ground an' see what the niggers 'ave 'id. They're a poor lot." Jakin stood upright on the branch and gazed across the plain.

"Lew," said he, "there's the Colonel coming. 'Colonel's a good old beggar. Let's go an' talk to 'im."

Lew nearly fell out of the tree at the audacity of the suggestion. Like Jakin he feared not God, neither regarded he Man, but there are limits even to the audacity of a drummer-boy, and to speak to a Colonel was—

But Jakin had slid down the trunk and doubled in the direction of the Colonel. That officer was walking wrapped in thought and visions of a C. B. yes, even a K. C. B., for had he not at command one of the best Regiments of the Line—the Fore and Fit? And he was aware of two small boys charging down upon him. Once before it had been solemnly reported to him that "the Drums were in a state of mutiny," Jakin and Lew being the ringleaders. This looked like an organised conspiracy.

The boys halted at twenty yards, walked to the regulation four paces, and saluted together, each as well set-up as a ramrod and little taller.

The Colonel was in a genial mood; the boys appeared very forlorn and unprotected on the desolate plain, and one of them was handsome.

"Well!" said the Colonel, recognising them. "Are you going to pull me down in the open? I'm sure I never interfere with you, even though"—he sniffed suspiciously—"you have been smoking."

It was time to strike while the iron was hot. Their hearts beat tumultuously.

"Beg y' pardon, Sir," began Jakin. "The Reg'ment's ordered on active service, Sir?"

"So I believe," said the Colonel courteously.

"Is the Band goin', Sir?" said both together. Then, without pause, "We're goin', Sir, ain't we?"

"You!" said the Colonel, stepping back the more fully to take in the two small figures. "You! You'd die in the first march."

"No, we wouldn't, Sir. We can march with the Reg'ment anywheres— p'rade an' anywhere else," said Jakin.

"If Tom Kidd goes 'e'll shut up like a clasp-knife," said Lew. "Tom 'as very-close veins in both 'is legs, Sir."

"Very how much?"

"Very-close veins, Sir. That's why they swells after long p'rade, Sir. If 'e can go, we can go, Sir."

Again the Colonel looked at them long and intently.

"Yes, the Band is going," he said as gravely as though he had been addressing a brother officer. "Have you any parents, either of you two?"

"No, Sir," rejoicingly from Lew and Jakin. "We're both orphans, Sir. There's no one to be considered of on our account, Sir."

"You poor little sprats, and you want to go up to the Front with the Regiment, do you? Why?"

"I've wore the Queen's Uniform for two years," said Jakin. "It's very 'ard, Sir, that a man don't get no recompense for doin' of 'is dooty, Sir."

"An'—an' if I don't go, Sir," interrupted Lew, "the Bandmaster 'e says 'e'll catch an' make a bloo—a blessed musician o' me, Sir. Before I've seen any service, Sir."

The Colonel made no answer for a long time. Then he said quietly: "If you're passed by the Doctor I dare say you can go. I shouldn't smoke if I were you."

The boys saluted and disappeared. The Colonel walked home and told the story to his wife, who nearly cried over it. The Colonel was well pleased. If that was the temper of the children, what would not the men do?

Jakin and Lew entered the boys' barrack-room with great stateliness, and refused to hold any conversation with their comrades for at least ten minutes. Then, bursting with pride, Jakin drawled: "I've bin intervooin' the Colonel. Good old beggar is the Colonel. Says I to 'im, 'Colonel,' says I, 'let me go to the Front, along o' the Reg'ment.—'To the Front you shall go,' says 'e, 'an' I only wish there was more like you among the dirty little devils that bang the bloomin' drums.' Kidd, if you throw your 'courtrements at me for tellin' you the truth to your own advantage, your legs'll swell."

None the less there was a Battle-Royal in the barrack-room, for the boys were consumed with envy and hate, and neither Jakin nor Lew behaved in conciliatory wise.

"I'm goin' out to say adoo to my girl," said Lew, to cap the climax. "Don't none o' you touch my kit because it's wanted for active service; me bein' specially invited to go by the Colonel."

He strolled forth and whistled in the clump of trees at the back of the Married Quarters till Cris came to him, and, the preliminary kisses being given and taken, Lew began to explain the situation.

"I'm goin' to the Front with the Reg'ment," he said valiantly.

"Piggy, you're a little liar," said Cris, but her heart misgave her, for Lew was not in the habit of lying.

"Liar yourself, Cris," said Lew, slipping an arm round her. "I'm goin'. When the Reg'ment marches out you'll see me with 'em, all galliant and gay. Give us another kiss, Cris, on the strength of it."

"If you'd on'y a-stayed at the Depot—where you ought to ha' bin—you could get as many of 'em as—as you dam please," whimpered Cris, putting up her mouth.

"It's 'ard, Cris. I grant you it's 'ard, But what's a man to do? If I'd a-stayed at the Depot, you wouldn't think anything of me."

"Like as not, but I'd 'ave you with me, Piggy. An' all the thinkin' in the world isn't like kissin'."

"An' all the kissin' in the world isn't like 'avin' a medal to wear on the front o' your coat."

"You won't get no medal."

"Oh, yus, I shall though. Me an' Jakin are the only acting-drummers that'll be took along. All the rest is full men, an' we'll get our medals with them."

"They might ha' taken anybody but you, Piggy. You'll get killed—you're so venturesome. Stay with me, Piggy darlin', down at the Depot, an' I'll love you true, for ever."

"Ain't you goin' to do that now, Cris? You said you was."

"O' course I am, but th' other's more comfortable. Wait till you've growed a bit, Piggy. You aren't no taller than me now."

"I've bin in the Army for two years, an' I'm not goin' to get out of a chanst o' seein' service, an' don't you try to make me do so. I'll come back, Cris, an' when I take on as a man I'll marry you—marry you when I'm a Lance."

"Promise, Piggy."

Lew reflected on the future as arranged by Jakin a short time previously, but Cris's mouth was very near to his own.

"I promise, s'elp me Gawd!" said he.

Cris slid an arm round his neck.

"I won't 'old you back no more, Piggy. Go away an' get your medal, an' I'll make you a new button-bag as nice as I know how," she whispered.

"Put some o' your 'air into it, Cris, an' I'll keep it in my pocket so long's I'm alive."

Then Cris wept anew, and the interview ended. Public feeling among the drummer-boys rose to fever pitch, and the lives of Jakin and Lew became unenviable. Not only had they been permitted to enlist two years before the regulation boy's age—fourteen—but, by virtue, it seemed, of their extreme youth, they were allowed to go to the Front—which thing had not happened to acting-drummers within the knowledge of boy. The Band which was to accompany the Regiment had been cut down to the regulation twenty men, the surplus returning to the ranks. Jakin and Lew were attached to the Band as supernumeraries, though they would much have preferred being company buglers.

"Don't matter much," said Jakin after the medical inspection. "Be thankful that we're 'lowed to go at all. The Doctor 'e said that if we could stand what we took from the Bazar-Sergeant's son we'd stand pretty nigh anything."

"Which we will," said Lew, looking tenderly at the ragged and ill-made housewife that Cris had given him, with a lock of her hair worked into a sprawling "L" upon the cover.

"It was the best I could," she sobbed. "I wouldn't let mother nor the Sergeant's tailor 'elp me. Keep it always, Piggy, an' remember I love you true."

They marched to the railway station, nine hundred and sixty strong, and every soul in cantonments turned out to see them go. The drummers gnashed their teeth at Jakin and Lew marching with the Band, the married women wept upon the platform, and the Regiment cheered its noble self black in the face.

"A nice level lot," said the Colonel to the Second-in-Command as they watched the first four companies entraining.

"Fit to do anything," said the Second-in-Command enthusiastically. "But it seems to me they're a thought too young and tender for the work in hand. It's bitter cold up at the Front now."

"They're sound enough," said the Colonel. "We must take our chance of sick casualties."

So they went northward, ever northward, past droves and droves of camels, armies of camp-followers, and legions of laden mules, the throng thickening day by day, till with a shriek the train pulled up at a hopelessly congested junction where six lines of temporary track accommodated six forty-waggon trains; where whistles blew, Babus sweated, and Commissariat officers swore from dawn till far into the night, amid the wind-driven chaff of the fodder-bales and the lowing of a thousand steers.

"Hurry up—you're badly wanted at the Front," was the message that greeted the Fore and Aft, and the occupants of the Red Cross carriages told the same tale.

"Tisn't so much the bloomin' fightin'," gasped a headbound trooper of Hussars to a knot of admiring Fore and Afts. "Tisn't so much the bloomin' fightin', though there's enough o' that. It's the bloomin' food an' the bloomin' climate. Frost all night 'cept when it hails, and b'iling sun all day, and the water stinks fit to knock you down. I got my 'ead chipped like a egg; I've got pneumonia too, an' my guts is all out o' order. 'Tain't no bloomin' picnic in those parts, I can tell you."

"Wot are the niggers like?" demanded a private.

"There's some prisoners in that train yonder. Go an' look at 'em. They're the aristocracy o' the country. The common folk are a dashed sight uglier. If you want to know what they fight with, reach under my seat an' pull out the long knife that's there."

They dragged out and beheld for the first time the grim, bone-handled, triangular Afghan knife. It was almost as long as Lew.

"That's the thing to j'int ye," said the trooper feebly. "It can take off a man's arm at the shoulder as easy as slicing butter. I halved the beggar that used that un, but there's more of his likes up above. They don't understand thrustin', but they're devils to slice."

The men strolled across the tracks to inspect the Afghan prisoners. They were unlike any "niggers" that the Fore and Aft had ever met—these huge, black-haired, scowling sons of the Beni-Israel. As the men stared the Afghans spat freely and muttered one to another with lowered eyes.

"My eyes! Wot awful swine!" said Jakin, who was in the rear of the procession. "Say, ole man, how you got puckrowed, eh? Kiswasti you wasn't hanged for your ugly face, hey?"

The tallest of the company turned, his leg-irons clanking at the movement, and stared at the boy. "See!" he cried to his fellows in Pushto. "They send children against us. What a people, and what fools!"

"Hya." said Jakin, nodding his head cheerily. "You go down-country. Khana get, peenikapanee get—live like a bloomin' Raja ke marfik. That's a better bandobust than baynit get it in your innards. Good-bye, ole man. Take care o' your beautiful figure'ead, an' try to look kushy."

The men laughed and fell in for their first march, when they began to realise that a soldier's life is not all beer and skittles. They were much impressed with the size and bestial ferocity of the niggers whom they had now learned to call "Paythans," and more with the exceeding discomfort of their own surroundings. Twenty old soldiers in the corps would have taught them how to make themselves moderately snug at night, but they had no old soldiers, and, as the troops on the line of march said, "they lived like pigs." They learned the heart-breaking cussedness of camp-kitchens and camels and the depravity of an E. P. tent and a wither-wrung mule. They studied animalculae in water, and developed a few cases of dysentery in their study.

At the end of their third march they were disagreeably surprised by the arrival in their camp of a hammered iron slug which, fired from a steady rest at seven hundred yards, flicked out the brains of a private seated by the fire. This robbed them of their peace for a night, and was the beginning of a long-range fire carefully calculated to that end. In the daytime they saw nothing except an unpleasant puff of smoke from a crag above the line of march. At night there were distant spurts of flame and occasional casualties, which set the whole camp blazing into the gloom and, occasionally, into opposite tents. Then they swore vehemently and vowed that this was magnificent but not war.

Indeed it was not. The Regiment could not halt for reprisals against the sharpshooters of the country-side. Its duty was to go forward and make connection with the Scotch and Goorkha troops with which it was brigaded. The Afghans knew this, and knew too, after their first tentative shots, that they were dealing with a raw regiment Thereafter they devoted themselves to the task of keeping the Fore and Aft on the strain. Not for anything would they have taken equal liberties with a seasoned corps—with the wicked little Goorkhas, whose delight it was to lie out in the open on a dark night and stalk their stalkers—with the terrible big men dressed in women's clothes, who could be heard praying to their God in the night-watches, and whose peace of mind no amount of "sniping" could shake— or with those vile Sikhs, who marched so ostentatiously unprepared and who dealt out such grim reward to those who tried to profit by that unpreparedness. This white regiment was different—quite different. It slept like a hog, and, like a hog, charged in every direction when it was roused. Its sentries walked with a footfall that could be heard for a quarter of a mile; would fire at anything that moved—even a driven donkey—and when they had once fired, could be scientifically "rushed" and laid out a horror and an offence against the morning sun. Then there were camp-followers who straggled and could be cut up without fear. Their shrieks would disturb the white boys, and the loss of their services would inconvenience them sorely.

Thus, at every march, the hidden enemy became bolder and the Regiment writhed and twisted under attacks it could not avenge. The crowning triumph was a sudden night-rush ending in the cutting of many tent-ropes, the collapse of the sodden canvas, and a glorious knifing of the men who struggled and kicked below. It was a great deed, neatly carried out, and it shook the already shaken nerves of the Fore and Aft. All the courage that they had been required to exercise up to this point was the "two o'clock in the morning courage"; and, so far, they had only succeeded in shooting their comrades and losing their sleep.

Sullen, discontented, cold, savage, sick, with their uniforms dulled and unclean, the Fore and Aft joined their Brigade.

"I hear you had a tough time of it coming up," said the Brigadier. But when he saw the hospital-sheets his face fell.

"This is bad," said he to himself. "They're as rotten as sheep." And aloud to the Colonel—"I'm afraid we can't spare you just yet. We want all we have, else I should have given you ten days to recover in."

The Colonel winced. "On my honour, Sir," he returned, "there is not the least necessity to think of sparing us. My men have been rather mauled and upset without a fair return. They only want to go in somewhere where they can see what's before them."

"Can't say I think much of the Fore and Fit," said the Brigadier in confidence to his Brigade-Major. "They've lost all their soldiering, and, by the trim of them, might have marched through the country from the other side. A more fagged-out set of men I never put eyes on."

"Oh, they'll improve as the work goes on. The parade gloss has been rubbed off a little, but they'll put on field polish before long," said the Brigade-Major. "They've been mauled, and they don't quite understand it."

They did not. All the hitting was on one side, and it was cruelly hard hitting with accessories that made them sick. There was also the real sickness that laid hold of a strong man and dragged him howling to the grave. Worst of all, their officers knew just as little of the country as the men themselves, and looked as if they did. The Fore and Aft were in a thoroughly unsatisfactory condition, but they believed that all would be well if they could once get a fair go-in at the enemy. Pot-shots up and down the valleys were unsatisfactory, and the bayonet never seemed to get a chance. Perhaps it was as well, for a long-limbed Afghan with a knife had a reach of eight feet, and could carry away lead that would disable three Englishmen.

The Fore and Aft would like some rifle-practice at the enemy—all seven hundred rifles blazing together. That wish showed the mood of the men.

The Goorkhas walked into their camp, and in broken, barrack-room English strove to fraternise with them: offered them pipes of tobacco and stood them treat at the canteen. But the Fore and Aft, not knowing much of the nature of the Goorkhas, treated them as they would treat any other "niggers," and the little men in green trotted back to their firm friends the Highlanders, and with many grins confided to them: "That dam white regiment no dam use. Sulky—ugh! Dirty—ugh! Hya, any tot for Johnny?" Whereat the Highlanders smote the Goorkhas as to the head, and told them not to vilify a British Regiment, and the Goorkhas grinned cavernously, for the Highlanders were their elder brothers and entitled to the privileges of kinship. The common soldier who touches a Goorkha is more than likely to have his head sliced open.

Three days later the Brigadier arranged a battle according to the rules of war and the peculiarity of the Afghan temperament. The enemy were massing in inconvenient strength among the hills, and the moving of many green standards warned him that the tribes were "up" in aid of the Afghan regular troops. A squadron and a half of Bengal Lancers represented the available Cavalry, and two screw-guns, borrowed from a column thirty miles away, the Artillery at the General's disposal.

"If they stand, as I've a very strong notion that they will, I fancy we shall see an infantry fight that will be worth watching," said the Brigadier. "We'll do it in style. Each regiment shall be played into action by its Band, and we'll hold the Cavalry in reserve."

"For all the reserve?" somebody asked.

"For all the reserve; because we're going to crumple them up," said the Brigadier, who was an extraordinary Brigadier, and did not believe in the value of a reserve when dealing with Asiatics. Indeed, when you come to think of it, had the British Army consistently waited for reserves in all its little affairs, the boundaries of Our Empire would have stopped at Brighton beach.

The battle was to be a glorious battle.

The three regiments debouching from three separate gorges, after duly crowning the heights above, were to converge from the centre, left, and right upon what we will call the Afghan army, then stationed towards the lower extremity of a flat-bottomed valley. Thus it will be seen that three sides of the valley practically belonged to the English, while the fourth was strictly Afghan property. In the event of defeat the Afghans had the rocky hills to fly to, where the fire from the guerrilla tribes in aid would cover their retreat. In the event of victory these same tribes would rush down and lend their weight to the rout of the British.

The screw-guns were to shell the head of each Afghan rush that was made in close formation, and the Cavalry, held in reserve in the right valley, were to gently stimulate the break-up which would follow on the combined attack. The Brigadier, sitting upon a rock overlooking the valley, would watch the battle unrolled at his feet. The Fore and Aft would debouch from the central gorge, the Goorkhas from the left, and the Highlanders from the right, for the reason that the left flank of the enemy seemed as though it required the most hammering. It was not every day that an Afghan force would take ground in the open, and the Brigadier was resolved to make the most of it.

"If we only had a few more men," he said plaintively, "we could surround the creatures and crumple 'em up thoroughly. As it is, I'm afraid we can only cut them up as they run. It's a great pity."

The Fore and Aft had enjoyed unbroken peace for five days, and were beginning, in spite of dysentery, to recover their nerve. But they were not happy, for they did not know the work in hand, and had they known, would not have known how to do it. Throughout those five days in which old soldiers might have taught them the craft of the game, they discussed together their misadventures in the past—how such an one was alive at dawn and dead ere the dusk, and with what shrieks and struggles such another had given up his soul under the Afghan knife. Death was a new and horrible thing to the sons of mechanics who were used to die decently of zymotic disease; and their careful conservation in barracks had done nothing to make them look upon it with less dread.

Very early in the dawn the bugles began to blow, and the Fore and Aft, filled with a misguided enthusiasm, turned out without waiting for a cup of coffee and a biscuit; and were rewarded by being kept under arms in the cold while the other regiments leisurely prepared for the fray. All the world knows that it is ill taking the breeks off a Highlander. It is much iller to try to make him stir unless he is convinced of the necessity for haste. 507 The Fore and Aft waited, leaning upon their rifles and listening to the protests of their empty stomachs. The Colonel did his best to remedy the default of lining as soon as it was borne in upon him that the affair would not begin at once, and so well did he succeed that the coffee was just ready when—the men moved off, their Band leading. Even then there had been a mistake in time, and the Fore and Aft came out into the valley ten minutes before the proper hour. Their Band wheeled to the right after reaching the open, and retired behind a little rocky knoll still playing while the Regiment went past.

It was not a pleasant sight that opened on the uninstructed view, for the lower end of the valley appeared to be filled by an army in position—real and actual regiments attired in red coats, and—of this there was no doubt—firing Martini-Henry bullets which cut up the ground a hundred yards in front of the leading company. Over that pock-marked ground the Regiment had to pass, and it opened the ball with a general and profound courtesy to the piping pickets; ducking in perfect time, as though it had been brazed on a rod. Being half capable of thinking for itself, it fired a volley by the simple process of pitching its rifle into its shoulder and pulling the trigger. The bullets may have accounted for some of the watchers on the hill side, but they certainly did not affect the mass of enemy in front, while the noise of the rifles drowned any orders that might have been given.

"Good God!" said the Brigadier, sitting on the rock high above all. "That Regiment has spoilt the whole show. Hurry up the others, and let the screw-guns get off."

But the screw-guns, in working round the heights, had stumbled upon a wasp's nest of a small mud fort which they incontinently shelled at eight hundred yards, to the huge discomfort of the occupants, who were unaccustomed to weapons of such devilish precision.

The Fore and Aft continued to go forward, but with shortened stride. Where were the other regiments, and why did these niggers use Martinis? They took open order instinctively, lying down and firing at random, rushing a few paces forward and lying down again, according to the regulations. Once in this formation, each man felt himself desperately alone, and edged in towards his fellow for comfort's sake.

Then the crack of his neighbor's rifle at his ear led him to fire as rapidly as he could—again for the sake of the comfort of the noise. The reward was not long delayed. Five volleys plunged the files in banked smoke impenetrable to the eye, and the bullets began to take ground twenty or thirty yards in front of the firers, as the weight of the bayonet dragged down and to the right arms wearied with holding the kick of the leaping Martini. The Company Commanders peered helplessly through the smoke, the more nervous mechanically trying to fan it away with their helmets.

"High and to the left!" bawled a Captain till he was hoarse. "No good! Cease firing, and let it drift away a bit."

Three and four times the bugles shrieked the order, and when it was obeyed the Fore and Aft looked that their foe should be lying before them in mown swaths of men. A light wind drove the smoke to leeward, and showed the enemy still in position and apparently unaffected. A quarter of a ton of lead had been buried a furlong in front of them, as the ragged earth attested.

That was not demoralizing to the Afghans, who have not European nerves. They were waiting for the mad riot to die down, and were firing quietly into the heart of the smoke. A private of the Fore and Aft spun up his company shrieking with agony, another was kicking the earth and gasping, and a third, ripped through the lower intestines by a jagged bullet, was calling aloud on his comrades to put him out of his pain. These were the casualties, and they were not soothing to hear or see. The smoke cleared to a dull haze.

Then the foe began to shout with a great shouting, and a mass—a black mass—detached itself from the main body, and rolled over the ground at horrid speed. It was composed of, perhaps, three hundred men, who would shout and fire and slash if the rush of their fifty comrades who were determined to die carried home. The fifty were Ghazis, half maddened with drugs and wholly mad with religious fanaticism. When they rushed the British fire ceased, and in the lull the order was given to close ranks and meet them with the bayonet.

Any one who knew the business could have told the Fore and Aft that the only way of dealing with a Ghazi rush is by volleys at long ranges; because a man who means to die, who desires to die, who will gain heaven by dying, must, in nine cases out of ten, kill a man who has a lingering prejudice in favour of life. Where they should have closed and gone forward, the Fore and Aft opened out and skirmished, and where they should have opened out and fired, they closed and waited.

A man dragged from his blankets half awake and unfed is never in a pleasant frame of mind. Nor does his happiness increase when he watches the whites of the eyes of three hundred six-foot fiends upon whose beards the foam is lying, upon whose tongues is a roar of wrath, and in whose hands are yard-long knives.

The Fore and Aft heard the Goorkha bugles bringing that regiment forward at the double, while the neighing of the Highland pipes came from the left. They strove to stay where they were, though the bayonets wavered down the line like the oars of a ragged boat. Then they felt body to body the amazing physical strength of their foes; a shriek of pain ended the rush, and the knives fell amid scenes not to be told. The men clubbed together and smote blindly—as often as not at their own fellows. Their front crumpled like paper, and the fifty Ghazis passed on; their backers, now drunk with success, fighting as madly as they.

Then the rear ranks were bidden to close up, and the subalterns dashed into the stew—alone. For the rear-ranks had heard the clamour in front, the yells and the howls of pain, and had seen the dark stale blood that makes afraid. They were not going to stay. It was the rushing of the camps over again. Let their officers go to Hell, if they chose; they would get away from the knives.

"Come on!" shrieked the subalterns, and their men, cursing them, drew back, each closing in to his neighbour and wheeling round.

Charteris and Devlin, subalterns of the last company, faced their death alone in the belief that their men would follow.

"You've killed me, you cowards," sobbed Devlin and dropped, cut from the shoulder-strap to the centre of the chest; and a fresh detachment of his men retreating, always retreating, trampled him under foot as they made for the pass whence they had emerged.

I kissed her in the kitchen and I kissed her in the hall Child'un, child'un, follow me! Oh Golly, said the cook, is he gwine to kiss us all? Halla— Halla—Halla—Hallelujah!

The Goorkhas were pouring through the left gorge and over the heights at the double to the invitation of their Regimental Quick-step. The black rocks were crowned with dark green spiders as the bugles gave tongue jubilantly:—

In the morning! In the morning by the bright light!

When Gabriel blows his trumpet in the morning!

The Goorkha rear companies tripped and blundered over loose stones. The front files halted for a moment to take stock of the valley and to settle stray boot-laces. Then a happy little sigh of contentment soughed down the ranks, and it was as though the land smiled, for behold there below was the enemy, and it was to meet them that the Goorkhas had doubled so hastily. There was much enemy. There would be amusement. The little men hitched their kukris well to hand, and gaped expectantly at their officers as terriers grin ere the stone is cast for them to fetch. The Goorkhas' ground sloped downward to the valley, and they enjoyed a fair view of the proceedings. They sat upon the boulders to watch, for their officers were not going to waste their wind in assisting to repulse a Ghazi rush more than half a mile away. Let the white men look to their own front.

"Hi! yi!" said the Subadar-Major, who was sweating profusely. "Dam fools yonder, stand close order! This is no time for close order, it is the time for volleys. Ugh!"

Horrified, amused, and indignant, the Goorkhas beheld the retirement of the Fore and Aft with a running chorus of oaths and commentaries.

"They run! The white men run! Colonel Sahib, may we also do a little running?" murmured Runbir Thappa, the Senior Jemadar.

But the Colonel would have none of it. "Let the beggars be cut up a little," said he wrathfully. "Serves 'em right. They'll be prodded into facing round in a minute." He looked through his field-glasses, and caught the glint of an officer's sword.

"Beating 'em with the flat—damned conscripts! How the Ghazis are walking into them!" said he.

The Fore and Aft, heading back, bore with them their officers. The narrowness of the pass forced the mob into solid formation, and the rear ranks delivered some sort of a wavering volley. The Ghazis drew off, for they did not know what reserve the gorge might hide. Moreover, it was never wise to chase white men too far. They returned as wolves return to cover, satisfied with the slaughter that they had done, and only stopping to slash at the wounded on the ground. A quarter of a mile had the Fore and Aft retreated, and now, jammed in the pass, was quivering with pain, shaken and demoralised with fear, while the officers, maddened beyond control, smote the men with the hilts and the flats of their swords.

"Get back! Get back, you cowards—you women! Right about face—column of companies, form—you hounds!" shouted the Colonel, and the subalterns swore aloud. But the Regiment wanted to go—to go anywhere out of the range of those merciless knives. It swayed to and fro irresolutely with shouts and outcries, while from the right the Goorkhas dropped volley after volley of cripple-stopper Snider bullets at long range into the mob of the Ghazis returning to their own troops.

The Fore and Aft Band, though protected from direct fire by the rocky knoll under which it had sat down, fled at the first rush. Jakin and Lew would have fled also, but their short legs left them fifty yards in the rear, and by the time the Band had mixed with the Regiment, they were painfully aware that they would have to close in alone and unsupported.

"Get back to that rock," gasped Jakin. "They won't see us there."

And they returned to the scattered instruments of the Band, their hearts nearly bursting their ribs.

"Here's a nice show for us," said Jakin, throwing himself full length on the ground. "A bloomin' fine show for British Infantry! Oh, the devils! They've gone and left us alone here! Wot'll we do?"

Lew took possession of a cast-off water-bottle, which naturally was full of canteen rum, and drank till he coughed again.

"Drink," said he shortly. "They'll come back in a minute or two—you see."

Jakin drank, but there was no sign of the Regiment's return. They could hear a dull clamour from the head of the valley of retreat, and saw the Ghazis slink back, quickening their pace as the Goorkhas fired at them.

"We're all that's left of the Band, an' we'll be cut up as sure as death," said Jakin.

"I'll die game, then," said Lew thickly, fumbling with his tiny drummer's sword. The drink was working on his brain as it was on Jakin's.

"'Old on! I know something better than fightin'," said Jakin, stung by the splendour of a sudden thought due chiefly to rum. "Tip our bloomin' cowards yonder the word to come back. The Paythan beggars are well away. Come on, Lew! We won't get hurt. Take the fife an' give me the drum. The Old Step for all your bloomin' guts are worth! There's a few of our men coming back now. Stand up, ye drunken little defaulter. By your right—quick march!"

He slipped the drum-sling over his shoulder, thrust the fife into Lew's hand, and the two boys marched out of the cover of the rock into the open, making a hideous hash of the first bars of the "British Grenadiers."

As Lew had said, a few of the Fore and Aft were coming back sullenly and shamefacedly under the stimulus of blows and abuse; their red coats shone at the head of the valley, and behind them were wavering bayonets. But between this shattered line and the enemy, who with Afghan suspicion feared that the hasty retreat meant an ambush, and had not moved therefore, lay half a mile of level ground dotted only by the wounded.

The tune settled into full swing and the boys kept shoulder to shoulder, Jakin banging the drum as one possessed. The one fife made a thin and pitiful squeaking, but the tune carried far, even to the Goorkhas.

"Come on, you dogs!" muttered Jakin to himself. "Are we to play forhever?" Lew was staring straight in front of him and marching more stiffly than ever he had done on parade.

And in bitter mockery of the distant mob, the old tune of the Old Line shrilled and rattled:—

> *Some talk of Alexander,*
>
> *And some of Hercules;*
>
> *Of Hector and Lysander,*
>
> *And such great names as these!*

There was a far-off clapping of hands from the Goorkhas, and a roar from the Highlanders in the distance, but never a shot was fired by British or Afghan. The two little red dots moved forward in the open parallel to the enemy's front.

> *But of all the world's great heroes*
>
> *There's none that can compare,*
>
> *With a tow-row-row-row-row-row,*
>
> *To the British Grenadier!*

The men of the Fore and Aft were gathering thick at the entrance into the plain. The Brigadier on the heights far above was speechless with rage. Still no movement from the enemy. The day stayed to watch the children.

Jakin halted and beat the long roll of the Assembly, while the fife squealed despairingly.

"Right about face! Hold up, Lew, you're drunk," said Jakin. They wheeled and marched back:—

> *'hose heroes of antiquity*
>
> *Ne'er saw a cannon-ball,*
>
> *Nor knew the force o' powder,*

"Here they come!" said Jakin. "Go on, Lew":—

> *To scare their foes withal!*

The Fore and Aft were pouring out of the valley. What officers had said to men in that time of shame and humiliation will never be known; for neither officers nor men speak of it now.

"They are coming anew!" shouted a priest among the Afghans. "Do not kill the boys! Take them alive, and they shall be of our faith."

But the first volley had been fired, and Lew dropped on his face. Jakin stood for a minute, spun round and collapsed, as the Fore and Aft came forward, the curses of their officers in their ears, and in their hearts the shame of open shame.

Half the men had seen the drummers die, and they made no sign. They did not even shout. They doubled out straight across the plain in open order, and they did not fire.

"This," said the Colonel of Goorkhas, softly, "is the real attack, as it should have been delivered. Come on, my children."

"Ulu-lu-lu-lu!" squealed the Goorkhas, and came down with a joyful clicking of kukris—those vicious Goorkha knives.

On the right there was no rush. The Highlanders, cannily commending their souls to God (for it matters as much to a dead man whether he has been shot in a Border scuffle or at Waterloo), opened out and fired according to their custom, that is to say without heat and without intervals, while the screw-guns, having disposed of the impertinent mud fort aforementioned, dropped shell after shell into the clusters round the flickering green standards on the heights.

"Charrging is an unfortunate necessity," murmured the Colour-Sergeant of the right company of the Highlanders. "It makes the men sweer so, but I am thinkin' that it will come to a charrge if these black devils stand much longer. Stewarrt, man, you're firing into the eye of the sun, and he'll not take any harm for Government ammuneetion. A foot lower and a great deal slower! What are the English doing? They're very quiet, there in the center. Running again?"

The English were not running. They were hacking and hewing and stabbing, for though one white man is seldom physically a match for an Afghan in a sheepskin or wadded coat, yet, through the pressure of many white men behind, and a certain thirst for revenge in his heart, he becomes capable of doing much with both ends of his rifle. The Fore and Aft held their fire till one bullet could drive through five or six men, and the front of the Afghan force gave on the volley. They then selected their men, and slew them with deep gasps and short hacking coughs, and groanings of leather belts against strained bodies, and realised for the first time that an Afghan attacked is far less formidable than an Afghan attacking; which fact old soldiers might have told them.

But they had no old soldiers in their ranks.

The Goorkhas' stall at the bazar was the noisiest, for the men were engaged—to a nasty noise as of beef being cut on the block—with the kukri, which they preferred to the bayonet; well knowing how the Afghan hates the half-moon blade.

As the Afghans wavered, the green standards on the mountain moved down to assist them in a last rally. This was unwise. The Lancers, chafing in the right gorge, had thrice despatched their only subaltern as galloper to report on the progress of affairs. On the third occasion he returned, with a bullet-graze on his knee, swearing strange oaths in Hindustani, and saying that all things were ready. So that squadron swung round the right of the Highlanders with a wicked whistling of wind in the pennons of its lances, and fell upon the remnant just when, according to all the rules of war, it should have waited for the foe to show more signs of wavering.

But it was a dainty charge, deftly delivered, and it ended by the Cavalry finding itself at the head of the pass by which the Afghans intended to retreat; and down the track that the lances had made streamed two companies of the Highlanders, which was never intended by the Brigadier. The new development was successful. It detached the enemy from his base as a sponge is torn from a rock, and left him ringed about with fire in that pitiless plain. And as a sponge is chased round the bath-tub by the hand of the bather, so were the Afghans chased till they broke into little detachments much more difficult to dispose of than large masses.

"See!" quoth the Brigadier. "Everything has come as I arranged. We've cut their base, and now we'll bucket 'em to pieces."

A direct hammering was all that the Brigadier had dared to hope for, considering the size of the force at his disposal; but men who stand or fall by the errors of their opponents may be forgiven for turning Chance into Design. The bucketing went forward merrily. The Afghan forces were upon the run—the run of wearied wolves who snarl and bite over their shoulders. The red lances dipped by twos and threes, and, with a shriek, uprose the lance-butt, like a spar on a stormy sea, as the trooper cantering forward cleared his point. The Lancers kept between their prey and the steep hills, for all who could were trying to escape from the valley of death. The Highlanders gave the fugitives two hundred yards' law, and then brought them down, gasping and choking ere they could reach the protection of the boulders above. The Goorkhas followed suit; but the Fore and Aft were killing on their own account, for they had penned a mass of men between their bayonets and a wall of rock, and the flash of the rifles was lighting the wadded coats.

"We cannot hold them, Captain Sahib!" panted a Ressaidar of Lancers. "Let us try the carbine. The lance is good, but it wastes time."

They tried the carbine, and still the enemy melted away—fled up the hills by hundreds when there were only twenty bullets to stop them. On the heights the screw-guns ceased firing—they had run out of ammunition— and the Brigadier groaned, for the musketry fire could not sufficiently smash the retreat. Long before the last volleys were fired, the doolies were out in force looking for the wounded. The battle was over, and, but for want of fresh troops, the Afghans would have been wiped off the earth. As it was, they counted their dead by hundreds, and nowhere were the dead thicker than in the track of the Fore and Aft.

But the Regiment did not cheer with the Highlanders, nor did they dance uncouth dances with the Goorkhas among the dead. They looked under their brows at the Colonel as they leaned upon their rifles and panted.

"Get back to camp, you. Haven't you disgraced yourself enough for one day! Go and look to the wounded. It's all you're fit for," said the Colonel. Yet for the past hour the Fore and Aft had been doing all that mortal commander could expect. They had lost heavily because they did not know how to set about their business with proper skill, but they had borne themselves gallantly, and this was their reward.

A young and sprightly Colour-Sergeant, who had begun to imagine himself a hero, offered his water-bottle to a Highlander whose tongue was black with thirst. "I drink with no cowards," answered the youngster huskily, and, turning to a Goorkha, said, "Hya, Johnny! Drink water got it?" The Goorkha grinned and passed his bottle. The Fore and Aft said no word.

They went back to camp when the field of strife had been a little mopped up and made presentable, and the Brigadier, who saw himself a Knight in three months, was the only soul who was complimentary to them. The Colonel was heartbroken, and the officers were savage and sullen.

"Well," said the Brigadier, "they are young troops, of course, and it was not unnatural that they should retire in disorder for a bit."

"Oh, my only Aunt Maria!" murmured a junior Staff Officer. "Retire in disorder! It was a bally run!"

"But they came again, as we all know," cooed the Brigadier, the Colonel's ashy-white face before him, "and they behaved as well as could possibly be expected. Behaved beautifully, indeed. I was watching them. It's not a matter to take to heart, Colonel. As some German General said of his men, they wanted to be shooted over a little, that was all." To himself he said—"Now they're blooded I can give 'em responsible work. It's as well that they got what they did. 'Teach 'em more than half a dozen rifle flirtations, that will—later—run alone and bite. Poor old Colonel, though."

All that afternoon the heliograph winked and flickered on the hills, striving to tell the good news to a mountain forty miles away And in the evening there arrived, dusty, sweating, and sore, a misguided Correspondent who had gone out to assist at a trumpery village-burning, and who had read off the message from afar, cursing his luck the while.

"Let's have the details somehow—as full as ever you can, please. It's the first time I've ever been left this campaign," said the Correspondent to the Brigadier; and the Brigadier, nothing loth, told him how an Army of Communication had been crumpled up, destroyed, and all but annihilated by the craft, strategy, wisdom, and foresight of the Brigadier.

But some say, and among these be the Goorkhas who watched on the hillside, that that battle was won by Jakin and Lew, whose little bodies were borne up just in time to fit two gaps at the head of the big ditch-grave for the dead under the heights of Jagai.

JUDSON AND THE EMPIRE

Gloriana! The Don may attack us

Whenever his stomach be fain;

He must reach us before he can rack us...

And where are the galleons of Spain?

Dobson.

One of the many beauties of a democracy is its almost superhuman skill in developing troubles with other countries and finding its honour abraded in the process. A true democracy has a large contempt for all other lands that are governed by Kings and Queens and Emperors, and knows little and thinks less of their internal affairs. All it regards is its own dignity, which is its King, Queen, and Knave. So, sooner or later, an international difference ends in the common people, who have no dignity, shouting the common abuse of the street, which also has no dignity, across the seas in order to vindicate their own dignity. The consequences may or may not be war, but the chances do not favour peace.

An advantage in living in a civilised land which is really governed lies in the fact that all the Kings and Queens and Emperors of the continent are closely related by blood or marriage—are, in fact, one large family. A wise head of them knows that what appears to be a studied insult may be no more than some man's indigestion or woman's indisposition to be treated as such, and explained in quiet talk. Again, a popular demonstration, headed by King and Court, may mean nothing more than that so-and-so's people are out of hand for the minute. When a horse falls to kicking in a hunt-crowd at a gate, the rider does not dismount, but puts his open hand behind him, and the others draw aside. It is so with the rulers of men. In the old days they cured their own and their people's bad temper with fire and slaughter; but now that the fire is so long of range and the slaughter so large, they do other things, and few among their people guess how much they owe in mere life and money to what the slang of the minute calls "puppets" and "luxuries."

Once upon a time there was a little Power, the half-bankrupt wreck of a once great empire, that lost its temper with England, the whipping-boy of all the world, and behaved, as every one knows, most scandalously. But it is not generally known that that Power fought a pitched battle with England

and won a glorious victory. The trouble began with the people. Their own misfortunes had been many, and for private rage it is always refreshing to find a vent in public swearing. Their national vanity had been deeply injured, and they thought of their ancient glories and the days when their fleets had first rounded the Cape of Storms, and their own newspapers called upon Camoens and urged them to extravagances. It was the gross, smooth, sleek, lying England that was checking their career of colonial expansion. They assumed at once that their ruler was in league with that country, and consequently they, his people, would forthwith become a Republic and colonially expand themselves as a free people should. This made plain, the people threw stones at the English Consuls and spat at English ladies, and cut off drunken sailors of our fleet in their ports and hammered them with oars, and made things very unpleasant for tourists at their customs, and threatened awful deaths to the consumptive invalids at Madeira, while the junior officers of the Army drank fruit-extracts and entered into blood-curdling conspiracies against their monarch, all with the object of being a Republic. Now the history of all the South American Republics shows that it is not good that Southern Europeans should be also Republicans. They glide too quickly into military despotism; and the propping of men against walls and shooting them in detachments can be arranged much more economically and with less effect on the death-rate by a hide-bound monarchy. Still the performances of the Power as represented by its people were extremely inconvenient. It was the kicking horse in the crowd, and probably the rider explained that he could not check it. The people enjoyed all the glory of war with none of the risks, and the tourists who were stoned in their travels returned stolidly to England and told the "Times" that the police arrangements of foreign towns were defective.

This then was the state of affairs north of the Line. South it was more strained, for there the Powers were at direct issue: England, unable to go back because of the pressure of adventurous children behind her, and the actions of far-away adventurers who would not come to heel, but offering to buy out her rival; and the other Power, lacking men or money, stiff in the conviction that three hundred years of slave-holding and intermingling with the nearest natives gave an inalienable right to hold slaves and issue half-castes to all eternity. They had built no roads. Their towns were rotting under their hands; they had no trade worth the freight of a crazy steamer, and their sovereignty ran almost one musket-shot inland when things were peaceful. For these very reasons they raged all the more, and the things that they said and wrote about the manners and customs of the English would have driven a younger nation to the guns with a long red bill for wounded honour.

It was then that Fate sent down in a twin-screw shallow-draft gunboat, designed for the defence of rivers, of some two hundred and seventy tons' displacement, Lieutenant Harrison Edward Judson, to be known for the future as Bai-Jove-Judson. His type of craft looked exactly like a flat-iron with a match stuck up in the middle; it drew five feet of water or less, carried a four-inch gun forward, which was trained by the ship, and, on account of its persistent rolling, was to live in three degrees worse than a torpedo-boat. When Judson was appointed to take charge of the thing on her little trip of six or seven thousand miles southward, his first remark as he went to look her over in dock was, "Bai Jove, that topmast wants staying forward!" The topmast was a stick about as thick as a clothes-prop, but the flat-iron was Judson's first command, and he would not have exchanged his position for second post on the "Anson" or the "Howe". He navigated her, under convoy, tenderly and lovingly to the Cape (the story of the topmast came with him), and he was so absurdly in love with his wallowing wash-tub when he reported himself, that the Admiral of the station thought it would be a pity to kill a new man on her, and allowed Judson to continue in his unenvied rule.

The Admiral visited her once in Simon's Bay, and she was bad, even for a flat-iron gunboat strictly designed for river and harbour defence. She sweated clammy drops of dew between decks in spite of a preparation of powdered cork that was sprinkled over her inside paint. She rolled in the long Cape swell like a buoy; her foc's'le was a dog-kennel; Judson's cabin was practically under the water-line; not one of her dead-bights could ever be opened; and her compasses, thanks to the influence of the four-inch gun, were a curiosity even among Admiralty compasses. But Bai-Jove-Judson was radiant and enthusiastic. He had even contrived to fill Mr. Davies, the second-class engine-room artificer, who was his chief engineer, with the glow of his passion. The Admiral, who remembered his own first command, when pride forbade him to slacken off a single rope on a dewy night, and he had racked his rigging to pieces in consequence, looked at the flat-iron keenly. Her fenders were done all over with white sennit which was truly white; her big gun was varnished with a better composition than the Admiralty allowed; the spare sights were cased as carefully as the chronometers; the chocks for spare spars, two of them, were made of four-inch Burma teak carved with dragons' heads that was one result of Bai-Jove-Judson's experiences with the Naval Brigade in the Burmese war; the bow-anchor was varnished instead of being painted, and there were charts more than the Admiralty scale supplied. The Admiral was well pleased, for he loved a ship's husband—a man who had a little money of his own and was willing to spend it on his command. Judson looked at him hopefully. He was only a Junior Navigating Lieutenant under eight years' standing. He might be kept in Simon's Bay for six months, and his ship at sea was his delight. The dream of his heart was to enliven her dismal official gray with a line of gold-leaf and perhaps a little scroll-work at her blunt barge-like bows.

"There's nothing like a first command, is there?" said the Admiral, reading his thoughts. "You seem to have rather queer compasses, though. Better get them adjusted."

"It's no use, sir," said Judson. "The gun would throw out the Pole itself. But—but I've got the hang of most of their weaknesses."

"Will you be good enough to lay that gun over thirty degrees, please?" The gun was put over. Round and round and round went the needle merrily, and the Admiral whistled.

"You must have kept close to your convoy?"

"Saw her twice between here and Madeira, sir," said Judson with a flush, for he resented the slur on his seamanship. "It's—it's a little out of hand, now, but she'll settle down after a while."

The Admiral went over the side, according to the rules of the Service, but the Staff-Captain must have told the other men of the squadron in Simon's Bay, for they one and all made light of the flat-iron for many days. "What can you shake out of her, Judson?" said the Lieutenant of the "Mongoose", a real white-painted, ram-bow gunboat with quick-firing guns, as he came into the upper verandah of the little naval Club overlooking the dockyard one hot afternoon. It is in that Club as the captains come and go that you hear all the gossip of all the Seven Seas.

"Ten point four," said Bai-Jove-Judson.

"Ah! That was on her trial trip. She's too deep by the head now. I told you staying that topmast would throw her out of trim."

"You leave my top-hamper alone," said Judson, for the joke was beginning to pall on him.

"Oh, my soul! Listen to him. Juddy's top-hamper! Keate, have you heard of the flat-iron's top-hamper? You're to leave it alone. Commodore Judson's feelings are hurt."

Keate was the Torpedo Lieutenant of the big "Vortigern", and he despised small things. "His top-hamper," said he slowly. "Oh, ah yes, of course. Juddy, there's a shoal of mullet in the bay, and I think they're foul of your screws. Better go down, or they'll carry away something."

"I don't let things carry away as a rule. You see I've no Torpedo Lieutenant on board, thank God!"

Keate within the past week had so managed to bungle the slinging in of a small torpedo-boat on the "Vortigern", that the boat had broken the crutches in which she rested, and was herself being repaired in the dockyard under the Club windows.

"One for you, Keate. Never mind, Juddy; you're hereby appointed dockyard-tender for the next three years, and if you're very good and there's no sea on, you shall take me round the harbour. Waitabeechee, Commodore. What'll you take? Vanderhum for the 'Cook and the captain bold, And the mate o' the Nancy brig, And the bo'sun tight' (Juddy, put that cue down or I'll put you under arrest for insulting the lieutenant of the real ship) 'And the midshipmite, And the crew of the captain's gig.'"

By this time Judson had pinned him in a corner, and was prodding him with the half-butt. The Admiral's Secretary entered, and saw the scuffle from afar.

"Ouch! Juddy, I apologise. Take that—er topmast of yours away! Here's the man with the bow-string. I wish I were a staff-captain instead of a bloody lootenant. Sperril sleeps below every night. That's what makes Sperril tumble home from the waist uppards. Sperril, I defy you to touch me. I'm under orders for Zanzibar. Probably I shall annex it!"

"Judson, the Admiral wants to see you!" said the Staff-Captain, disregarding the scoffer of the "Mongoose".

"I told you you'd be a dockyard-tender yet, Juddy. A side of fresh beef to-morrow and three dozen snapper on ice. On ice, you understand, Juddy?"

Bai-Jove-Judson and the Staff-Captain went out together.

"Now, what does the Admiral want with Judson?" said Keate from the bar.

"Don't know. Juddy's a damned good fellow, though. I wish to goodness he was on the Mongoose with us."

The Lieutenant of the "Mongoose" dropped into a chair and read the mail papers for an hour. Then he saw Bai-Jove-Judson in the street and shouted to him. Judson's eyes were very bright, and his figure was held very straight, and he moved joyously. Except for the Lieutenant of the "Mongoose", the Club was empty.

"Juddy, there will be a beautiful row," said that young man when he had heard the news delivered in an undertone. "You'll probably have to fight, and yet I can't see what the Admiral's thinking of to—"

"My orders are not to fight under any circumstances," said Judson.

"Go-look-see? That all? When do you go?"

"To-night if I can. I must go down and see about things. I say, I may want a few men for the day."

"Anything on the 'Mongoose' is at your service. There's my gig come in now. I know that coast, dead, drunk, or asleep, and you'll need all the knowledge you can get. If it had only been us two together! Come over with me!"

For one whole hour Judson remained closeted in the stern cabin of the "Mongoose", listening, poring over chart upon chart and taking notes, and for an hour the marine at the door heard nothing but things like these: "Now you'll have to put in here if there's any sea on. That current is ridiculously under-estimated, and it sets west at this season of the year, remember. Their boats never come south of this, see? So it's no good looking out for them." And so on and so forth, while Judson lay at length on the locker by the three-pounder, and smoked and absorbed it all.

Next morning there was no flat-iron in Simon's Bay, only a little smudge of smoke off Cape Hangklip to show that Mr. Davies, the second-class engine-room artificer, was giving her all she could carry. At the Admiral's house, the ancient and retired bo'sun, who had seen many Admirals come and go, brought out his paint and brushes and gave a new coat of pure raw pea-green to the two big cannon-balls that stood one on each side of the Admiral's entrance-gate. He felt dimly that great events were stirring.

And the flat-iron, constructed, as has been before said, solely for the defense of rivers, met the great roll off Cape Agulhas and was swept from end to end and sat upon her twin-screws and leaped as gracefully as a cow in a bog from one sea to another, till Mr. Davies began to fear for the safety of his engines, and the Kroo boys that made the majority of the crew were deathly sick. She ran along a very badly-lighted coast, past bays that were no bays, where ugly flat-topped rocks lay almost level with the water, and very many extraordinary things happened that have nothing to do with the story, but they were all duly logged by Bai-Jove-Judson.

At last the coast changed and grew green and low and exceedingly muddy, and there were broad rivers whose bars were little islands standing three or four miles out at sea, and Bai-Jove-Judson hugged the shore more closely than ever, remembering what the Lieutenant of the "Mongoose" had told him. Then he found a river full of the smell of fever and mud, with green stuff growing far into its waters, and a current that made the flatiron gasp and grunt.

"We will turn up here," said Bai-Jove-Judson, and they turned up accordingly; Mr. Davies wondering what in the world it all meant, and the

Kroo boys grinning. Bai-Jove-Judson went forward to the bows and meditated, staring through the muddy waters. After six hours of rooting through this desolation at an average rate of five miles an hour, his eyes were cheered by the sight of one white buoy in the coffee-hued mid-stream. The flat-iron crept up to it cautiously, and a leadsman took soundings all around it from a dinghy, while Bai-Jove-Judson smoked and thought, with his head on one side.

"About seven feet, isn't there?" said he. "That must be the tail end of the shoal. There's four fathom in the fairway. Knock that buoy down with axes. I don't think it's picturesque somehow." The Kroo men hacked the wooden sides to pieces in three minutes, and the mooring-chain sank with the lasst splinters of wood. Bai-Jove Judson laid the flat-iron carefully over the site, while Mr. Davies watched, biting his nails nervously.

"Can you back her against this current?" said Bai-Jove-Judson. Mr. Davies could, inch by inch, but only inch by inch, and Bai-Jove-Judson sat in the bows and gazed at various things on the bank as they came into line or opened out. The flatiron dropped down over the tail of the shoal, exactly where the buoy had been, and backed once before Bai-Jove-Judson was satisfied. Then they went up stream for half an hour, put into shoal water by the bank and waited, with a slip-rope on the anchor.

"Seems to me," said Mr. Davies deferentially, "like as if I heard some one a-firing off at intervals, so to say."

There was beyond doubt a dull mutter in the air. "Seems to me," said Bai-Jove-Judson, "as if I heard a screw. Stand by to slip her moorings."

Another ten minutes passed and the beat of engines grew plainer. Then round the bend of the river came a remarkably prettily built white-painted gunboat with a blue and white flag bearing a red boss in the centre.

"Unshackle abaft the windlass! Stream both buoys! Easy, astern. Let go, all!" The slip-rope flew out, the two buoys bobbed in the water to mark where anchor and cable had been left, and the flat-iron waddled out into midstream with the white ensign at her one mast-head.

"Give her all you can. That thing has the legs of us," said Judson. "And down we go!"

"It's war—bloody war. He's going to fire," said Mr. Davies, looking up through the engine-room hatch.

The white gunboat without a word of explanation fired three guns at the flat-iron, cutting the trees on the banks into green chips. Bai-Jove-Judson was at the wheel, and Mr. Davies and the current helped the boat to an almost respectable degree of speed.

It was an exciting chase, but it did not last for more than five minutes. The white gunboat fired again, and Mr. Davies in his engine-room gave a wild shout.

"What's the matter? Hit?" said Bai-Jove-Judson.

"No, I've just seized of your roos-de-gare. Beg y' pardon, sir."

"Right O! Just the half a fraction of a point more." The wheel turned under the steady hand, as Bai-Jove-Judson watched his marks on the bank coming in line swiftly as troops anxious to aid. The flat-iron smelt the shoal water under her, checked for an instant, and went on. "Now we're over. Come along, you thieves, there!"

The white gunboat, too hurried even to fire, was storming in the wake of the flat-iron, steering as she steered. This was unfortunate, because the lighter craft was dead over the missing buoy.

"What you do here?" shouted a voice from the bows.

"I'm going on. Hold tight. Now you're arranged for!"

There was a crash and a clatter as the white gunboat's nose took the shoal, and the brown mud boiled up in oozy circles under her forefoot. Then the current caught her stem by the starboard side and drove her broadside on to the shoal, slowly and gracefully. There she heeled at an undignified angle, and her crew yelled aloud.

"Neat! Oh, damn neat!" quoth Mr. Davies, dancing on the engine-room plates, while the Kroo stokers grinned.

The flat-iron turned up-stream again, and passed under the hove-up starboard side of the white gunboat, to be received with howls and imprecations in a strange tongue. The stranded boat, exposed even to her lower strakes, was as defence-less as a turtle on its back, without the advantage of the turtle's plating. And the one big blunt gun in the bows of the flat-iron was unpleasantly near.

But the captain was valiant and swore mightily. Bai-Jove-Judson took no sort of notice. His business was to go up the river.

"We will come in a flotilla of boats and ecrazer your vile tricks," said the captain with language that need not be published.

Then said Bai-Jove-Judson, who was a linguist: "You stay o where you are o, or I'll leave a hole-o in your bottom o that will make you much os perforatados."

There was a great deal of mixed language in reply, but Bai-Jove-Judson was out of hearing in a few minutes, and Mr. Davies, himself a man of few words, confided to one of his subordinates that Lieutenant Judson was "a most remarkable prompt officer in a way of putting it."

For two hours the flat-iron pawed madly through the muddy water, and that which had been at first a mutter became a distinct rumble.

"Was war declared?" said Mr. Davies, and Bai-Jove-Judson laughed. "Then, damn his eyes, he might have spoilt my pretty little engines. There's war up there, though."

The next bend brought them full in sight of a small but lively village, built round a whitewashed mud house of some pretensions. There were scores and scores of saddle-coloured soldiery on duty, white uniforms running to and fro and shouting round a man in a litter, and on a gentle slope that ran inland for four or five miles something like a brisk battle was raging round a rude stockade. A smell of unburied carcasses floated through the air and vexed the sensitive nose of Mr. Davies, who spat over the side.

"I want to get this gun on that house," said Bai-Jove-Judson, indicating the superior dwelling over whose flat roof floated the blue and white flag. The little twin screws kicked up the water exactly as a hen's legs kick in the dust before she settles down to a bath. The little boat moved un easily from left to right, backed, yawed again, went ahead, and at last the gray blunt gun's nose was held as straight as a rifle-barrel on the mark indicated. Then Mr. Davies allowed the whistle to speak as it is not allowed to speak in Her Majesty's service on account of waste of steam. The soldiery of the village gathered into knots and groups and bunches, and the firing up the hill ceased, and every one except the crew of the flatiron yelled aloud. Something like an English cheer came down wind.

"Our chaps in mischief for sure, probably," said Mr. Davies. "They must have declared war weeks ago, in a kind of way, seems to me."

"Hold her steady, you son of a soldier!" shouted Bai-Jove-Judson, as the muzzle fell off the white house.

Something rang as loudly as a ship's bell on the forward plates of the flat-iron, something spluttered in the water, and another thing cut a groove in the deck planking an inch in front of Bai-Jove-Judson's left foot. The saddle-coloured soldiery were firing as the mood took them, and the man in the litter waved a shining sword. The muzzle of the big gun kicked down a fraction as it was laid on the mud wall at the bottom of the house garden. Ten pounds of gunpowder shut up in a hundred pounds of metal was its charge. Three or four yards of the mud wall jumped up a little, as a man jumps when he is caught in the small of the back with a knee-cap, and then fell forward, spreading fan-wise in the fall. The soldiery fired no more that day, and Judson saw an old black woman climb to the flat roof of the house. She fumbled for a time with the flag halliards, then finding that they were jammed, took off her one garment, which happened to be an Isabella-coloured petticoat, and waved it impatiently. The man in the litter flourished a white handkerchief, and Bai-Jove-Judson grinned. "Now we'll give 'em one up the hill. Round with her, Mr. Davies. Curse the man who invented those floating gun platforms. Where can I pitch in a notice without slaying one of those little devils?"

The side of the slope was speckled with men returning in a disorderly fashion to the river front. Behind them marched a small but very compact body of men who had filed out of the stockade. These last dragged quick-firing guns with them.

"Bai Jove, it's a regular army. I wonder whose," said Bai-Jove-Judson, and he waited developments. The descending troops met and mixed with the troops in the village, and, with the litter in the centre, crowded down to the river, till the men with the quick-firing guns came up behind them. Then they divided left and right and the detachment marched through.

"Heave these damned things over!" said the leader of the party, and one after another ten little gatlings splashed into the muddy water. The flatiron lay close to the bank.

"When you're quite done," said Bai-Jove-Judson politely, "would you mind telling me what's the matter? I'm in charge here."

"We're the Pioneers of the General Development Company," said the leader. "These little bounders have been hammering us in lager for twelve hours, and we're getting rid of their gatlings. Had to climb out and take them; but they've snaffled the lock-actions. Glad to see you."

"Any one hurt?"

"No one killed exactly, but we're very dry."

"Can you hold your men?"

The man turned round and looked at his command with a grin. There were seventy of them, all dusty and unkempt.

"We sha'n't sack this ash-bin, if that's what you mean. We're mostly gentlemen here, though we don't look it."

"All right. Send the head of this post, or fort, or village, or whatever it is, aboard, and make what arrangements you can for your men."

"We'll find some barrack accommodation somewhere. Hullo! You in the litter there, go aboard the gunboat." The command wheeled round, pushed through the dislocated soldiery, and began to search through the village for spare huts.

The little man in the litter came aboard smiling nervously. He was in the fullest of full uniform, with many yards of gold lace and dangling chains. Also he wore very large spurs; the nearest horse being not more than four hundred miles away. "My children," said he, facing the silent soldiery, "lay aside your arms."

Most of the men had dropped them already and were sitting down to smoke. "Let nothing," he added in his own tongue, "tempt you to kill these who have sought your protection."

"Now," said Bai-Jove-Judson, on whom the last remark was lost, "will you have the goodness to explain what the deuce you mean by all this nonsense?"

"It was of a necessitate," said the little man. "The operations of war are unconformible. I am the Governor and I operate Captain. Be'old my little sword."

"Confound your little sword, sir. I don't want it. You've fired on our flag. You've been firing at our people here for a week, and I've been fired at coming up the river."

"Ah! The 'Guadala'. She have misconstrued you for a slaver possibly. How are the 'Guadala'?"

"Mistook a ship of Her Majesty's navy for a slaver! You mistake any craft for a slaver! Bai Jove, sir, I've a good mind to hang you at the yard-arm!"

There was nothing nearer that terrible spar than the walking-stick in the rack of Judson's cabin. The Governor looked at the one mast and smiled a deprecating smile.

"The position is embarrassment," he said. "Captain, do you think those illustrious traders burn my capital? My people will give them beer."

"Never mind the traders, I want an explanation."

"Hum! There are popular uprising in Europe, Captain—in my country." His eye wandered aimlessly round the horizon.

"What has that to do with—"

"Captain, you are very young. There is still uproariment. But!"—here he slapped his chest till his epaulets jingled—"I am loyalist to pits of all my stomachs."

"Go on," said Judson, and his mouth quivered.

"An order arrive to me to establish a custom-houses here, and to collect of the taximent from the traders when she are come here necessarily. That was on account of political understandings with your country and mine. But on that arrangement there was no money also. Not one damn little cowrie. I desire damnably to extend all commercial things, and why? I am loyalist and there is rebellion—yes, I tell you—Republics in my country for to just begin. You do not believe? See some time how it exist. I cannot make this custom-houses and pay the so high-paid officials. The people too in my country they say the king she has no regardance into Honour of her nation. He throw away everything—Gladstone her all, you say, pay?"

"Yes, that's what we say," said Judson with a grin.

"Therefore they say, let us be Republics on hot cakes. But I—I am loyalist to all my hands' ends. Captain, once I was attache at Mexico. I say the Republics are no good. The peoples have her stomach high. They desire—they desire—a course for the bills."

"What on earth is that?"

"The cock-fight for pay at the gate. You give something, pay for see bloody row. Do I make its comprehension?"

"A run for their money—is that what you mean? Gad, you're sporting, Governor."

"So I say. I am loyalist, too." He smiled more easily. "Now how can anything do herself for the customs-houses; but when the Company's mens she arrives, then a cock-fight for pay at gate that is quite correct. My army he says it will Republic and shoot me off upon walls if I have not give her blood. An army, Captain, are terrible in her angries—especialment when she are not paid. I know, too," here he laid his hand on Judson's shoulder, "I know too we are old friends. Yes! Badajos, Almeida, Fuentes d'Onor— time ever since; and a little, little cock-fight for pay at gate that is good for my king. More sit her tight on throne behind, you see? Now," he waved his hand round the decayed village, "I say to my armies, Fight! Fight the Company's men when she come, but fight not so very strong that you are any deads. It is all in the raporta that I send. But you understand, Captain, we are good friends all the time. Ah! Ciudad Rodrigo, you remember? No? Perhaps your father, then? So you see no one are deads, and we fight a fight, and it is all in the raporta, to please the people in our country, and my armies they do not put me against the walls. You see?"

"Yes; but the 'Guadala'. She fired on us. Was that part of your game, my joker?"

"The 'Guadala'. Ah! No, I think not. Her captain he is too big fool. But I think she have gone down the coast. Those your gunboats poke her nose and shove her oar in every place. How is 'Guadala'?"

"On a shoal. Stuck till I take her off." "There are any deads?"

"No."

The Governor drew a breath of deep relief. "There are no deads here. So you see none are deads anywhere, and nothing is done. Captain, you talk to the Company's mens. I think they are not pleased."

"Naturally."

"They have no sense. I thought to go backwards again they would. I leave her stockade alone all night to let them out, but they stay and come facewards to me, not backwards. They did not know we must conquer much in all these battles, or the king, he is kicked off her throne. Now we have won this battle—this great battle," he waved his arms abroad, "and I think you will say so that we have won, Captain. You are loyalist also. You would not disturb to the peaceful Europe? Captain, I tell you this. Your Queen she know too. She would not fight her cousins. It is a—a hand-up thing."

"What?"

"Hand-up thing. Jobe you put. How you say?"

"Put-up job?"

"Yes. Put-up job. Who is hurt? We win. You lose. All righta?"

Bai-Jove-Judson had been exploding at intervals for the last five minutes. Here he broke down completely and roared aloud.

"But look here, Governor," he said at last, "I've got to think of other things than your riots in Europe. You've fired on our flag."

"Captain, if you are me, you would have done how? And also, and also," he drew himself up to his full height, "we are both brave men of bravest countries. Our honour is the honour of our King," here he uncovered, "and of our Queen," here he bowed low. "Now, Captain, you shall shell my palace and I shall be your prisoner."

"Skittles!" said Bai-Jove-Judson. "I can't shell that old hencoop."

"Then come to dinner. Madeira, she are still to us, and I have of the best she manufac."

He skipped over the side beaming, and Bai-Jove-Judson went into the cabin to laugh his laugh out. When he had recovered a little he sent Mr.

Davies to the head of the Pioneers, the dusty man with the gatlings, and the troops who had abandoned the pursuit of arms watched the disgraceful spectacle of two men reeling with laughter on the quarter-deck of a gunboat.

"I'll put my men to build him a custom-house," said the head of the Pioneers, gasping. "We'll make him one decent road at least. That Governor ought to be knighted. I'm glad now that we didn't fight 'em in the open, or we'd have killed some of them. So he's won great battles, has he? Give him the compliments of the victims, and tell him I'm coming to dinner. You haven't such a thing as a dress-suit, have you? I haven't seen one for six months."

That evening there was a dinner in the village—a general and enthusiastic dinner, whose head was in the Governor's house, and whose tail threshed at large throughout all the streets. The Madeira was everything that the Governor had said, and more, and it was tested against two or three bottles of Bai-Jove-Judson's best Vanderhum, which is Cape brandy ten years in the bottle, flavoured with orange-peel and spices. Before the coffee was removed (by the lady who had made the flag of truce) the Governor had sold the whole of his governorship and its appurtenances, once to Bai-Jove-Judson for services rendered by Judson's grandfather in the Peninsular War, and once to the head of the Pioneers, in consideration of that gentleman's good friendship. After the negotiation he retreated for a while into an inner apartment, and there evolved a true and complete account of the defeat of the British arms, which he read with his cocked hat over one eye to Judson and his companion. It was Judson who suggested the sinking of the flat-iron with all hands, and the head of the Pioneers who supplied the list of killed and wounded (not more than two hundred) in his command.

"Gentlemen," said the Governor from under his cocked hat, "the peace of Europe are saved by this raporta. You shall all be Knights of the Golden Hide. She shall go by the 'Guadala'."

"Great Heavens!" said Bai-Jove Judson, flushed but composed, "that reminds me I've left that boat stuck on her broadside down the river. I must go down and soothe the commandante. He'll be blue with rage. Governor, let us go a sail on the river to cool our heads. A picnic, you understand."

"Ya—as, everything I understand. Ho! A picnica! You are all my prisoner, but I am good gaoler. We shall picnic on the river, and we shall take all the girls. Come on, my prisoners."

"I do hope," said the head of the Pioneers, staring from the verandah into the roaring village, "that my chaps won't set the town alight by accident. Hullo! Hullo! A guard of honour for His Excellency the most illustrious Governor!"

Some thirty men answered the call, made a swaying line upon a more swaying course, and bore the Governor most swayingly of all high in the arms as they staggered down to the river. And the song that they sang bade them, "Swing, swing together their body between their knees"; and they obeyed the words of the song faithfully, except that they were anything but "steady from stroke to bow." His Excellency the Governor slept on his uneasy litter, and did not wake when the chorus dropped him on the deck of the flat-iron.

"Good-night and good-bye," said the head of the Pioneers to Judson; "I'd give you my card if I had it, but I'm so damned drunk I hardly know my own club. Oh, yes! It's the Travellers. If ever we meet in Town, remember me. I must stay here and look after my fellows. We're all right in the open, now. I s'pose you'll return the Governor some time. This is a political crisis. Good-night."

The flat-iron went down stream through the dark. The Governor slept on deck, and Judson took the wheel, but how he steered, and why he did not run into each bank many times, that officer does not remember. Mr. Davies did not note anything unusual, for there are two ways of taking too much, and Judson was only ward-room, not foc's'le drunk. As the night grew colder the Governor woke up, and expressed a desire for whiskey and soda. When that came they were nearly abreast of the stranded "Guadala", and His Excellency saluted the flag that he could not see with loyal and patriotic strains.

"They do not see. They do not hear," he cried. "Ten thousand saints! They sleep, and I have won battles! Ha!"

He started forward to the gun, which, very naturally, was loaded, pulled the lanyard, and woke the dead night with the roar of the full charge behind a common shell. That shell mercifully just missed the stern of the "Guadala", and burst on the bank. "Now you shall salute your Governor," said he, as he heard feet running in all directions within the iron skin. "Why you demand so base a quarter? I am here with all my prisoners."

In the hurly-burly and the general shriek for mercy his reassurances were not heard.

"Captain," said a grave voice from the ship, "we have surrendered. Is it the custom of the English to fire on a helpless ship'?"

"Surrendered! Holy Virgin! I go to cut off all their heads. You shall be ate by wild ants—flogged and drowned. Throw me a balcony. It is I, the Governor! You shall never surrender. Judson of my soul, ascend her insides, and send me a bed, for I am sleepy; but, oh, I will multiple time kill that captain!"

"Oh!" said the voice in the darkness, "I begin to comprehend." And a rope-ladder was thrown, up which the Governor scrambled, with Judson at his heels.

"Now we will enjoy executions," said the Governor on the deck. "All these Republicans shall be shot. Little Judson, if I am not drunk, why are so sloping the boards which do not support?"

The deck, as I have said, was at a very stiff cant. His Excellency sat down, slid to leeward, and was asleep again.

The captain of the "Guadala" bit his moustache furiously, and muttered in his own tongue: "This land is the father of great villains and the stepfather of honest men. You see our material, Captain. It is so everywhere with us. You have killed some of the rats, I hope?"

"Not a rat," said Judson genially.

"That is a pity. If they were dead, our country might send us men; but our country is dead too, and I am dishonoured on a mud-bank through your English treachery."

"Well, it seems to me that firing on a little tub of our size without a word of warning, when you know that the countries were at peace, is treachery enough in a small way."

"If one of my guns had touched you, you would have gone to the bottom, all of you. I would have taken the risk with my Government. By that time it would have been—"

"A Republic? So you really did mean fighting on your own hook? You're rather a dangerous officer to cut loose in a navy like yours. Well, what are you going to do now?"

"Stay here. Go away in boats. What does it matter? That drunken cat"— he pointed to the shadow in which the Governor slept—"is here. I must take him back to his hole."

"Very good. I'll tow you off at daylight if you get steam ready."

"Captain, I warn you that as soon as she floats again I will fight you."

"Humbug! You'll have lunch with me, and then you'll take the Governor up the river."

The captain was silent for some time. Then he said: "Let us drink. What must be, must be; and after all we have not forgotten the Peninsula. You will admit, Captain, that it is bad to be run upon a shoal like a mud-dredger?"

"Oh, we'll pull you off before you can say knife. Take care of His Excellency. I shall try to get a little sleep now."

They slept on both ships till the morning, and then the work of towing off the "Guadala" began. With the help of her own engines, and the tugging and puffing of the flat-iron, she slid off the mud-bank sideways into the deep water, the flatiron immediately under her stern, and the big eye of the four-inch gun almost peering through the window of the captain's cabin.

Remorse in the shape of a violent headache had overtaken the Governor. He was uneasily conscious that he might, perhaps, have exceeded his powers; and the captain of the "Guadala", in spite of all his patriotic sentiments, remembered distinctly that no war had been declared between the two countries. He did not need the Governor's repeated reminders that war, serious war, meant a Republic at home, possible supersession in his command, and much shooting of living men against dead walls.

"We have satisfied our honour," said the Governor in confidence. "Our army is appeased, and the raporta that you take home will show that we were loyal and brave. That other captain? Bah! he is a boy. He will call this a—a-. Judson of my soul, how you say this is—all this affairs which have transpired between us?"

Judson was watching the last hawser slipping through the fairlead. "Call it? Oh, I should call it rather a lark. Now your boat's all right, Captain. When will you come to lunch?"

"I told you," said the Governor, "it would be a larque to him."

"Mother of the Saints! then what is his seriousness?" said the captain. "We shall be happy to come when you please. Indeed, we have no other choice," he added bitterly.

"Not at all," said Judson, and as he looked at the three or four shot-blisters on the bows of his boat a brilliant idea took him. "It is we who are at your mercy. See how His Excellency's guns knocked us about."

"Senior Captain," said the Governor pityingly, "that is very sad. You are most injured, and your deck too, it is all shot over. We shall not be too severe on a beat man, shall we, Captain?"

"You couldn't spare us a little paint, could you? I'd like to patch up a little after the—action," said Judson meditatively, fingering his upper lip to hide a smile.

"Our store-room is at your disposition," said the captain of the "Guadala", and his eye brightened; for a few lead splashes on gray paint make a big show.

"Mr. Davies, go aboard and see what they have to spare—to spare, remember. Their spar-colour with a little working up should be just our freeboard tint."

"Oh, yes. I'll spare them," said Mr. Davies savagely. "I don't understand this how-d'you-do and damn-your-eyes business coming one atop of the other in a manner o' speaking. By all rights, they're our lawful prize."

The Governor and the captain came to lunch in the absence of Mr. Davies. Bai-Jove-Judson had not much to offer, but what he had was given as by a beaten foeman to a generous conqueror. When they were a little warmed—the Governor genial and the captain almost effusive—he explained, quite casually, over the opening of a bottle that it would not be to his interest to report the affair seriously, and it was in the highest degree improbable that the Admiral would treat it in any grave fashion.

"When my decks are cut up" (there was one groove across four planks), "and my plates buckled" (there were five lead patches on three plates), "and I meet such a boat as the 'Guadala', and a mere accident saves me from being blown out of the water—"

"Yes. A mere accident, Captain. The shoal-buoy has been lost," said the captain of the 'Guadala'.

"Ah? I do not know this river. That was very sad. But as I was saying, when an accident saves me from being sunk, what can I do but go away—if that is possible? But I fear that I have no coal for the sea voyage. It is very sad." Judson had compromised on what he knew of the French tongue as a working language.

"It is enough," said the Governor, waving a generous hand. "Judson of my soul, the coal is yours, and you shall be repaired—yes, repaired all over of your battle's wounds. You shall go with all the honours of all the wars. Your flag shall fly. Your drum shall beat. Your, ah!—jolly boys shall spoke their bayonets. Is it not so, Captain?"

"As you say, Excellency. But the traders in the town. What of them?"

The Governor looked puzzled for an instant. He could not quite remember what had happened to those jovial men who had cheered him over night. Judson interrupted swiftly: "His Excellency has set them to forced works on barracks and magazines, and, I think, a custom-house. When that is done they will be released, I hope, Excellency."

"Yes, they shall be released for your sake, little Judson of my heart." Then they drank the health of their respective sovereigns, while Mr. Davies superintended the removal of the scarred plank and the shot-marks on the deck and the bow-plates.

"Oh, this is too bad," said Judson when they went on deck. "That idiot has exceeded his instructions, but—but yow must let me pay for this!"

Mr. Davies, his legs in the water as he sat on a staging slung over the bows, was acutely conscious that he was being blamed in a foreign tongue. He smiled uneasily, and went on with his work.

"What is it?" said the Governor.

"That thick-head has thought that we needed some gold-leaf, and he has borrowed that from your storeroom, but I must make it good." Then in English, "Stand up, Mr. Davies. What the—in—do you mean by taking their gold-leaf? My—, are we a set of pirates to scrape the guts out of a Levantine bumboat? Look contrite, you butt-ended, broad-breeched, bottle-bellied, swivel-eyed son of a tinker, you! My Soul alive, can't I maintain discipline in my own ship without a blacksmith of a boiler-riveter putting me to shame before a yellow-nosed picaroon. Get off the staging, Mr. Davies, and go to the engine-room. Put down that leaf first, though, and leave the books where they are. I'll send for you in a minute. Go aft!"

Now, only the upper half of Mr. Davies's round face was above the bulwarks when this torrent of abuse descended upon him; and it rose inch by inch as the shower continued: blank amazement, bewilderment, rage, and injured pride chasing each other across it till he saw his superior officer's left eyelid flutter on the cheek twice. Then he fled to the engine-room, and wiping his brow with a handful of cotton-waste, sat down to overtake circumstances.

"I am desolated," said Judson to his companions, "but you see the material that you give us. This leaves me more in your debt than before. The stuff I can replace" (gold-leaf is never carried on floating gun-platforms), "but for the insolence of that man how shall I apologise?"

Mr. Davies's mind moved slowly, but after a while he transferred the cotton-waste from his forehead to his mouth and bit on it to prevent laughter. He began a second dance on the engine-room plates. "Neat! Oh, damned neat!" he chuckled. "I've served with a good few, but there never was one so neat as him. And I thought he was the new kind that don't know how to put a few words, as it were!"

"Mr. Davies, you can continue your work," said Judson down the engine-room hatch. "These officers have been good enough to speak in your favour. Make a thorough job of it while you are about it. Slap on every man you have. Where did you get hold of it?"

"Their storeroom is a regular theatre, sir. You couldn't miss it. There's enough for two first-rates, and I've scoffed the best half of it."

"Look sharp, then. We shall be coaling from her this afternoon. You'll have to cover it all."

"Neat! Oh, damned neat!" said Mr. Davies under his breath, as he gathered his subordinates together, and set about accomplishing the long-deferred wish of Judson's heart.

It was the "Martin Frobisher", the flag-ship, a great war-boat when she was new, in the days when men built for sail as well as for steam. She could turn twelve knots under full sail, and it was under that that she stood up the mouth of the river, a pyramid of silver beneath the moon. The Admiral, fearing that he had given Judson a task beyond his strength, was coming to look for him, and incidentally to do a little diplomatic work along the coast. There was hardly wind enough to move the "Frobisher" a couple of knots an hour, and the silence of the land closed about her as she entered the fairway. Her yards sighed a little from time to time, and the ripple under her bows answered the sigh. The full moon rose over the steaming swamps, and the Admiral, gazing upon it, thought less of Judson and more of the softer emotions. In answer to the very mood of his mind, there floated across the silver levels of the water, mellowed by distance to a most poignant sweetness, the throb of a mandolin, and the voice of one who called upon a genteel Julia—upon Julia, and upon love. The song ceased, and the sighing of the yards was all that broke the silence of the big ship.

Again the mandolin began, and the commander on the lee side of the quarter-deck grinned a grin that was reflected in the face of the signal-midshipman. Not a word of the song was lost, and the voice of the singer was the voice of Judson.

"Last week down our alley came a toff,

Nice old geyser with a nasty cough,

Sees my missus, takes his topper off,

Quite in a gentlemanly way "—

and so on to the end of the verse. The chorus was borne by several voices, and the signal-midshipman's foot began to tap the deck furtively.

"'What cheer!' all the neighbours cried.

"Oo are you going to meet, Bill?

'Ave you bought the street, Bill?'

Laugh?—I thought I should ha' died

When I knocked 'em in the old Kent Road."

It was the Admiral's gig, rowing softly, that came into the midst of that merry little smoking-concert. It was Judson, the beribboned mandolin round his neck, who received the Admiral as he came up the side of the "Guadala", and it may or may not have been the Admiral who stayed till two in the morning and delighted the hearts of the Captain and the Governor. He had come as an unbidden guest, and he departed as an honoured one, but strictly unofficial throughout. Judson told his tale next day in the Admiral's cabin as well as he could in the face of the Admiral's gales of laughter, but the most amazing tale was that told by Mr. Davies to his friends in the dockyard at Simon's Town from the point of view of a second-class engine-room artificer, all unversed in diplomacy.

And if there be no truth either in my tale, which is Judson's tale, or the tale of Mr. Davies, you will not find in harbour at Simon's Town to-day a flat-bottomed twin-screw gunboat, designed solely for the defence of rivers, about two hundred and seventy tons' displacement and five feet draught, wearing in open defiance of the rules of the Service a gold line on her gray paint. It follows also that you will be compelled to credit that version of the fray which, signed by His Excellency the Governor and despatched in the "Guadala", satisfied the self-love of a great and glorious people, and saved a monarchy from the ill-considered despotism which is called a Republic.

A CONFERENCE OF THE POWERS

Life liveth but in life, and doth not roam

To other lands if all be well at home:

"Solid as ocean foam," quoth ocean foam.

The room was blue with the smoke of three pipes and a cigar. The leave-season had opened in India, and the first-fruits on this side of the water were "Tick" Boileau, of the 45th Bengal Cavalry, who called on me, after three years' absence, to discuss old things which had happened. Fate, who always does her work handsomely, sent up the same staircase within the same hour The Infant, fresh from Upper Burma, and he and Boileau looking out of my window saw walking in the street one Nevin, late in a Goorkha regiment which had been through the Black Mountain Expedition. They yelled to him to come up, and the whole Street was aware that they desired him to come up, and he came up, and there followed Pandemonium in my room because we had foregathered from the ends of the earth, and three of us were on a holiday, and none of us were twenty-five, and all the delights of all London lay waiting our pleasure.

Boileau took the only other chair, The Infant, by right of his bulk, the sofa; and Nevin, being a little man, sat cross-legged on the top of the revolving bookcase, and we all said, "Who'd ha' thought it!" and "What are you doing here?" till speculation was exhausted and the talk went over to inevitable "shop." Boileau was full of a great scheme for winning a military attache-ship at St. Petersburg; Nevin had hopes of the Staff College, and The Infant had been moving heaven and earth and the Horse Guards for a commission in the Egyptian army.

"What's the use o' that?" said Nevin, twirling round on the bookcase.

"Oh, heaps! 'Course if you get stuck with a Fellaheen regiment, you're sold; but if you are appointed to a Soudanese lot, you're in clover. They are first-class fighting-men—and just think of the eligible central position of Egypt in the next row!"

This was putting the match to a magazine. We all began to explain the Central Asian question off-hand, flinging army corps from the Helmund to Kashmir with more than Russian recklessness. Each of the boys made for himself a war to his own liking, and when we had settled all the details of Armageddon, killed all our senior officers, handled a division apiece, and nearly torn the atlas in two in attempts to explain our theories, Boileau needs must lift up his voice above the clamour, and cry, "Anyhow it'll be the hell of a row!" in tones that carried conviction far down the staircase.

Entered, unperceived in the smoke, William the Silent. "Gen'elman to see you, sir," said he, and disappeared, leaving in his stead none other than Mr. Eustace Cleever. William would have introduced the Dragon of Wantley with equal disregard of present company.

"I—I beg your pardon. I didn't know that there was anybody—with you.—"

But it was not seemly to allow Mr. Cleever to depart; he was a great man. The boys remained where they were, for any movement would have choked up the little room. Only when they saw his gray hairs they stood on their feet, and when The Infant caught the name, he said:

"Are you—did you write that book called 'As it was in the Beginning'?"

Mr. Cleever admitted that he had written the book.

"Then—then I don't know how to thank you, sir," said The Infant, flushing pink. "I was brought up in the country you wrote about—all my people live there; and I read the book in camp on the Hlinedatalone, and I knew every stick and stone, and the dialect too; and, by Jove! it was just like being at home and hearing the country people talk. Nevin, you know 'As it was in the Beginning'? So does Ti—Boileau."

Mr. Cleever has tasted as much praise, public and private, as one man may safely swallow; but it seemed to me that the outspoken admiration in The Infant's eyes and the little stir in the little company came home to him very nearly indeed.

"Won't you take the sofa?" said The Infant. "I'll sit on Boileau's chair, and—" here he looked at me to spur me to my duties as a host; but I was watching the novelist's face. Cleever had not the least intention of going away, but settled himself on the sofa.

Following the first great law of the Army, which says "all property is common except money, and you've only got to ask the next man for that," The Infant offered tobacco and drink. It was the least he could do; but not the most lavish praise in the world held half as much appreciation and reverence as The Infant's simple "Say when, sir," above the long glass.

Cleever said "when," and more thereto, for he was a golden talker, and he sat in the midst of hero-worship devoid of all taint of self-interest. The boys asked him of the birth of his book, and whether it was hard to write, and how his notions came to him; and he answered with the same absolute simplicity as he was questioned. His big eyes twinkled, he dug his long thin hands into his gray beard and tugged it as he grew animated. He dropped little by little from the peculiar pinching of the broader vowels—the indefinable "euh," that runs through the speech of the pundit caste—and the elaborate choice of words, to freely-mouthed "ows" and "ois," and, for him at least, unfettered colloquialisms. He could not altogether understand the boys, who hung upon his words so reverently. The line of the chinstrap, that still showed white and untanned on cheekbone and jaw, the steadfast young eyes puckered at the corners of the lids with much staring through red-hot sunshine, the slow, untroubled breathing, and the curious, crisp, curt speech seemed to puzzle him equally. He could create men and women, and send them to the uttermost ends of the earth, to help, delight, and comfort; he knew every mood of the fields, and could interpret them to the cities, and he knew the hearts of many in city and country, but he had hardly, in forty years, come into contact with the thing which is called a Subaltern of the Line. He told the boys this in his own way.

"Well, how should you?" said The Infant. "You—you're quite different, y' see, sir."

The Infant expressed his ideas in his tone rather than his words, but Cleever understood the compliment.

"We're only Subs," said Nevin, "and we aren't exactly the sort of men you'd meet much in your life, I s'pose."

"That's true," said Cleever. "I live chiefly among men who write, and paint, and sculp, and so forth. We have our own talk and our own interests, and the outer world doesn't trouble us much."

"That must be awfully jolly," said Boileau, at a venture. "We have our own shop, too, but 'tisn't half as interesting as yours, of course. You know all the men who've ever done anything; and we only knock about from place to place, and we do nothing."

"The Army's a very lazy profession if you choose to make it so," said Nevin. "When there's nothing going on, there is nothing going on, and you lie up."

"Or try to get a billet somewhere, to be ready for the next show," said The Infant with a chuckle.

"To me," said Cleever softly, "the whole idea of warfare seems so foreign and unnatural, so essentially vulgar, if I may say so, that I can hardly appreciate your sensations. Of course, though, any change from idling in garrison towns must be a godsend to you."

Like many home-staying Englishmen, Cleever believed that the newspaper phrase he quoted covered the whole duty of the Army whose toils enabled him to enjoy his many-sided life in peace. The remark was not a happy one, for Boileau had just come off the Frontier, The Infant had been on the warpath for nearly eighteen months, and the little red man Nevin two months before had been sleeping under the stars at the peril of his life. But none of them tried to explain, till I ventured to point out that they had all seen service and were not used to idling. Cleever took in the idea slowly.

"Seen service?" said he. Then, as a child might ask, "Tell me. Tell me everything about everything."

"How do you mean?" said The Infant, delighted at being directly appealed to by the great man.

"Good Heavens! How am I to make you understand, if you can't see. In the first place, what is your age?"

"Twenty-three next July," said The Infant promptly.

Cleever questioned the others with his eyes.

"I'm twenty-four," said Nevin.

"And I'm twenty-two," said Boileau.

"And you've all seen service?"

"We've all knocked about a little bit, sir, but The Infant's the war-worn veteran. He's had two years' work in Upper Burma," said Nevin.

"When you say work, what do you mean, you extraordinary creatures?"

"Explain it, Infant," said Nevin.

"Oh, keeping things in order generally, and running about after little dakus—that's dacoits—and so on. There's nothing to explain."

"Make that young Leviathan speak," said Cleever impatiently, above his glass.

"How can he speak?" said I. "He's done the work. The two don't go together. But, Infant, you're ordered to bukb."

"What about? I'll try."

"Bukb about a daur. You've been on heaps of 'em," said Nevin.

"What in the world does that mean? Has the Army a language of its own?"

The Infant turned very red. He was afraid he was being laughed at, and he detested talking before outsiders; but it was the author of "As it was in the Beginning" who waited.

"It's all so new to me," pleaded Cleever; "and—and you said you liked my book."

This was a direct appeal that The Infant could understand, and he began rather flurriedly, with much slang bred of nervousness—

"Pull me up, sir, if I say anything you don't follow. About six months before I took my leave out of Burma, I was on the Hlinedatalone, up near the Shan States, with sixty Tommies—private soldiers, that is—and another subaltern, a year senior to me. The Burmese business was a subaltern's war, and our forces were split up into little detachments, all running about the country and trying to keep the dacoits quiet. The dacoits were having a first-class time, y' know—filling women up with kerosene and setting 'em alight, and burning villages, and crucifying people."

The wonder in Eustace Cleever's eyes deepened. He could not quite realise that the cross still existed in any form.

"Have you ever seen a crucifixion?" said he.

"Of course not. 'Shouldn't have allowed it if I had; but I've seen the corpses. The dacoits had a trick of sending a crucified corpse down the river on a raft, just to show they were keeping their tail up and enjoying themselves. Well, that was the kind of people I had to deal with."

"Alone?" said Cleever. Solitude of the soul he could understand—none better—but he had never in the body moved ten miles from his fellows.

"I had my men, but the rest of it was pretty much alone. The nearest post that could give me orders was fifteen miles away, and we used to heliograph to them, and they used to give us orders same way—too many orders."

"Who was your C. O.?" said Boileau.

"Bounderby—Major. Pukka Bounderby; more Bounder than pukka. He went out up Bhamo way. Shot, or cut down, last year," said The Infant.

"What are these interludes in a strange tongue?" said Cleever to me.

"Professional information—like the Mississippi pilots' talk," said I. "He did not approve of his major, who died a violent death. Go on, Infant."

"Far too many orders. You couldn't take the Tommies out for a two days' daur—that's expedition—without being blown up for not asking leave. And the whole country was humming with dacoits. I used to send out spies, and act on their information. As soon as a man came in and told me of a gang in hiding, I'd take thirty men with some grub, and go out and look for them, while the other subaltern lay doggo in camp."

"Lay! Pardon me, but how did he lie?" said Cleever.

"Lay doggo—lay quiet, with the other thirty men. When I came back, he'd take out his half of the men, and have a good time of his own."

"Who was he?" said Boileau.

"Carter-Deecey, of the Aurungabadis. Good chap, but too zubberdusty, and went bokhar four days out of seven. He's gone out too. Don't interrupt a man."

Cleever looked helplessly at me.

"The other subaltern," I translated swiftly, "came from a native regiment, and was overbearing in his demeanour. He suffered much from the fever of the country, and is now dead. Go on, Infant."

"After a bit, we got into trouble for using the men on frivolous occasions, and so I used to put my signaller under arrest to prevent him reading the helio-orders. Then I'd go out and leave a message to be sent an hour after I got clear of the camp, something like this: 'Received important information; start in an hour, unless countermanded.' If I was ordered back, it didn't much matter. I swore the C. O.'s watch was wrong, or something, when I came back. The Tommies enjoyed the fun, and—Oh, yes, there was one Tommy who was the bard of the detachment. He used to make up verses on everything that happened."

"What sort of verses?" said Cleever.

"Lovely verses; and the Tommies used to sing 'em. There was one song with a chorus, and it said something like this." The Infant dropped into the true barrack-room twang:

"Theebaw, the Burma king, did a very foolish thing, When 'e mustered 'ostile forces in ar-rai, 'E little thought that we, from far across the sea, Would send our armies up to Mandalai!"

"O gorgeous!" said Cleever. "And how magnificently direct! The notion of a regimental bard is new to me, but of course it must be so."

"He was awfly popular with the men," said The Infant. "He had them all down in rhyme as soon as ever they had done anything. He was a great bard. He was always ready with an elegy when we picked up a Boh—that's a leader of dacoits."

"How did you pick him up?" said Cleever.

"Oh! shot him if he wouldn't surrender."

"You! Have you shot a man?"

There was a subdued chuckle from all three boys, and it dawned on the questioner that one experience in life which was denied to himself, and he weighed the souls of men in a balance, had been shared by three very young gentlemen of engaging appearance. He turned round on Nevin, who had climbed to the top of the bookcase and was sitting cross-legged as before.

"And have you, too?"

"Think so," said Nevin, sweetly. "In the Black Mountain. He was rolling cliffs on to my half-company, and spoiling our formation. I took a rifle from a man, and brought him down at the second shot."

"Good Heavens! And how did you feel afterwards?"

"Thirsty. I wanted a smoke, too."

Cleever looked at Boileau—the youngest. Surely his hands were guiltless of blood.

Boileau shook his head and laughed. "Go on, Infant," said he.

"And you too?" said Cleever.

"Fancy so. It was a case of cut, cut or be cut, with me; so I cut—one. I couldn't do any more, sir."

Cleever looked as though he would like to ask many questions, but The Infant swept on in the full tide of his tale.

"Well, we were called insubordinate young whelps at last, and strictly forbidden to take the Tommies out any more without orders. I wasn't sorry, because Tommy is such an exacting sort of creature. He wants to live as though he were in barracks all the time. I was grubbing on fowls and boiled corn, but the Tommies wanted their pound of fresh meat, and their half ounce of this, and their two ounces of t'other thing, and they used to come to me and badger me for plug tobacco when we were four days in jungle. I said: 'I can get you Burma tobacco, but I don't keep a canteen up my sleeve.' They couldn't see it. They wanted all the luxuries of the season, confound 'em!"

"You were alone when you were dealing with these men?" said Cleever, watching The Infant's face under the palm of his hand. He was receiving new ideas, and they seemed to trouble him.

"Of course, unless you count the mosquitoes. They were nearly as big as the men. After I had to lie doggo I began to look for something to do, and

I was great pals with a man called Hicksey in the Police, the best man that ever stepped on earth; a first-class man."

Cleever nodded applause. He knew how to appreciate enthusiasm.

"Hicksey and I were as thick as thieves. He had some Burma mounted police—rummy chaps, armed with sword and Snider carbine. They rode punchy Burma ponies, with string stirrups, red cloth saddles, and red bell-rope headstalls. Hicksey used to lend me six or eight of them when I asked him—nippy little devils, keen as mustard. But they told their wives too much, and all my plans got known, till I learned to give false marching orders overnight, and take the men to quite a different village in the morning. Then we used to catch the simple daku before breakfast, and made him very sick. It's a ghastly country on the Hlinedatalone; all bamboo jungle, with paths about four feet wide winding through it. The daku knew all the paths, and potted at us as we came round a corner; but the mounted police knew the paths as well as the daku, and we used to go stalking 'em in and out. Once we flushed 'em, the men on the ponies had the advantage of the men on foot. We held all the country absolutely quiet for ten miles round, in about a month. Then we took Boh Na-ghee, Hicksey and I and the civil officer. That was a lark!"

"I think I am beginning to understand a little," said Cleever. "It was a pleasure to you to administer and fight?"

"Rather! There's nothing nicer than a satisfactory little expedition, when you find your plans fit together, and your information's teek—correct, you know, and the whole sub-chiz—I mean, when everything works out like formulae on a blackboard. Hicksey had all the information about the Boh. He had been burning villages and murdering people right and left, and cutting up Government convoys, and all that. He was lying doggo in a village about fifteen miles off, waiting to get a fresh gang together. So we arranged to take thirty mounted police, and turn him out before he could plunder into our newly-settled villages. At the last minute, the civil officer in our part of the world thought he'd assist at the performance."

"Who was he?" said Nevin.

"His name was Dennis," said The Infant slowly. "And we'll let it stay so. He's a better man now than he was then."

"But how old was the civil power?" said Cleever. "The situation is developing itself."

"He was about six-and-twenty, and he was awf'ly clever. He knew a lot of things, but I don't think he was quite steady enough for dacoit-hunting. We started overnight for Boh Na-ghee's village, and we got there just before morning, without raising an alarm. Dennis had turned out armed to his teeth—two revolvers, a carbine, and all sorts of things. I was talking to Hicksey about posting the men, and Dennis edged his pony in between us, and said, 'What shall I do? What shall I do? Tell me what to do, you fellows.' We didn't take much notice; but his pony tried to bite me in the leg, and I said, 'Pull out a bit, old man, till we've settled the attack.' He kept edging in, and fiddling with his reins and his revolvers, and saying, 'Dear me! Dear me! Oh, dear me! What do you think I'd better do?' The man was in a deadly funk, and his teeth were chattering."

"I sympathise with the civil power," said Cleever. "Continue, young Clive."

"The fun of it was, that he was supposed to be our superior officer. Hicksey took a good look at him, and told him to attach himself to my party. Beastly mean of Hicksey, that. The chap kept on edging in and bothering, instead of asking for some men and taking up his own position, till I got angry, and the carbines began popping on the other side of the village. Then I said, 'For God's sake be quiet, and sit down where you are! If you see anybody come out of the village, shoot at him.' I knew he couldn't hit a hayrick at a yard. Then I took my men over the garden wall— over the palisades, y' know—somehow or other, and the fun began. Hicksey had found the Boh in bed under a mosquito-curtain, and he had taken a flying jump on to him."

"A flying jump!" said Cleever. "Is that also war?"

"Yes," said The Infant, now thoroughly warmed. "Don't you know how you take a flying jump on to a fellow's head at school, when he snores in the dormitory? The Boh was sleeping in a bedful of swords and pistols, and Hicksey came down like Zazel through the netting, and the net got mixed up with the pistols and the Boh and Hicksey, and they all rolled on the floor together. I laughed till I couldn't stand, and Hicksey was cursing me for not helping him; so I left him to fight it out and went into the village. Our men were slashing about and firing, and so were the dacoits, and in the thick of the mess some ass set fire to a house, and we all had to clear out. I froze on to the nearest daku and ran to the palisade, shoving him in front of me. He wriggled loose and bounded over the other side. I came after him; but when I had one leg one side and one leg the other of the palisade, I saw that the daku had fallen flat on Dennis's head. That man had never moved from where I left him. They rolled on the ground together, and Dennis's carbine went off and nearly shot me. The daku picked himself up and ran, and Dennis buzzed his carbine after him, and it caught him on the back of his head and knocked him silly. You never saw anything so funny in your life. I doubled up on the top of the palisade and hung there, yelling with laughter. But Dennis began to weep like anything. 'Oh, I've killed a man,' he said. 'I've killed a man, and I shall never know another peaceful hour in my life. Is he dead? Oh, is he dead? Good Lord, I've killed a man!' I came down and said, 'Don't be a fool;' but he kept on shouting, 'Is he dead?' till I could have kicked him. The daku was only knocked out of time with the carbine. He came to after a bit, and I said, 'Are you hurt much?' He groaned and said, 'No.' His chest was all cut with scrambling over the palisade. 'The white man's gun didn't do that,' he said; 'I did that, and I knocked the white man over.' Just like a Burman, wasn't it? But Dennis wouldn't be happy at any price. He said: 'Tie up his wounds. He'll bleed to death. Oh, he'll bleed to death!' 'Tie 'em up yourself,' I said, 'if you're so anxious.' 'I can't touch him,' said Dennis, 'but here's my shirt.' He took off his shirt, and fixed the braces again over his bare shoulders. I ripped the shirt up, and bandaged the dacoit quite professionally. He was grinning at Dennis all the time; and Dennis's haversack was lying on the ground, bursting full of sandwiches. Greedy hog! I took some, and offered some to Dennis. 'How can I eat?' he said. 'How can you ask me to eat? His very blood is on your hands now, and you're eating my sandwiches!' 'All right,' I said; 'I'll give 'em to the daku.' So I did, and the little chap was quite pleased, and wolfed 'em down like one o'clock."

Cleever brought his hand down on the table with a thump that made the empty glasses dance. "That's Art!" he said. "Flat, flagrant mechanism! Don't tell me that happened on the spot!"

The pupils of The Infant's eyes contracted to two pin-points. "I beg your pardon," he said slowly and stiffly, "but I am telling this thing as it happened."

Cleever looked at him a moment. "My fault entirely," said he; "I should have known. Please go on."

"Hicksey came out of what was left of the village with his prisoners and captives, all neatly tied up. Boh Na-ghee was first, and one of the villagers, as soon as he found the old ruffian helpless, began kicking him quietly. The Boh stood it as long as he could, and then groaned, and we saw what was going on. Hicksey tied the villager up and gave him a half a dozen, good, with a bamboo, to remind him to leave a prisoner alone. You should have seen the old Boh grin. Oh! but Hicksey was in a furious rage with everybody. He'd got a wipe over the elbow that had tickled up his funny-bone, and he was rabid with me for not having helped him with the Boh and the mosquito-net. I had to explain that I couldn't do anything. If you'd seen 'em both tangled up together on the floor in one kicking cocoon, you'd have laughed for a week. Hicksey swore that the only decent man of his acquaintance was the Boh, and all the way to camp Hicksey was talking to the Boh, and the Boh was complaining about the soreness of his bones. When we got back, and had had a bath, the Boh wanted to know when he was going to be hanged. Hicksey said he couldn't oblige him on the spot, but had to send him to Rangoon. The Boh went down on his knees, and reeled off a catalogue of his crimes—he ought to have been hanged seventeen times over, by his own confession—and implored Hicksey to settle the business out of hand. 'If I'm sent to Rangoon,' said he, 'they'll keep me in jail all my life, and that is a death every time the sun gets up or the wind blows.' But we had to send him to Rangoon, and, of course, he was let off down there, and given penal servitude for life. When I came to Rangoon I went over the jail—I had helped to fill it, y' know—and the old Boh was there, and he spotted me at once. He begged for some opium first, and I tried to get him some, but that was against the rules. Then he asked me to have his Sentence changed to death, because he was afraid of being sent to the Andamans. I couldn't do that either, but I tried to cheer him, and told him how things were going up-country, and the last thing he said was—'Give my compliments to the fat white man who jumped on me. If I'd been awake I'd have killed him.' I wrote that to Hicksey next mail, and—and that's all. I'm 'fraid I've been gassing awf'ly, sir."

Cleever said nothing for a long time. The Infant looked uncomfortable. He feared that, misled by enthusiasm, he had filled up the novelist's time with unprofitable recital of trivial anecdotes.

Then said Cleever, "I can't understand. Why should you have seen and done all these things before you have cut your wisdom-teeth?"

"Don't know," said The Infant apologetically. "I haven't seen much—only Burmese jungle."

"And dead men, and war, and power, and responsibility," said Cleever, under his breath. "You won't have any sensations left at thirty, if you go on as you have done. But I want to hear more tales—more tales!" He seemed to forget that even subalterns might have engagements of their own.

"We're thinking of dining out somewhere—the lot of us—and going on to the Empire afterwards," said Nevin, with hesitation. He did not like to ask Cleever to come too. The invitation might be regarded as perilously near to "cheek." And Cleever, anxious not to wag a gray beard unbidden among boys at large, said nothing on his side.

Boileau solved the little difficulty by blurting out: "Won't you come too, sir?"

Cleever almost shouted "Yes," and while he was being helped into his coat continued to murmur "Good Heavens!" at intervals in a way that the boys could not understand.

"I don't think I've been to the Empire in my life," said he; "but—what is my life after all? Let us go."

They went out with Eustace Cleever, and I sulked at home because they had come to see me, but had gone over to the better man; which was humiliating. They packed him into a cab with utmost reverence, for was he not the author of "As it was in the Beginning," and a person in whose company it was an honour to go abroad? From all I gathered later, he had taken less interest in the performance before him than in their conversations, and they protested with emphasis that he was "as good a man as they make; knew what a man was driving at almost before he said it; and yet he's so damned simple about things any man knows." That was one of many comments.

At midnight they returned, announcing that they were "highly respectable gondoliers," and that oysters and stout were what they chiefly needed. The eminent novelist was still with them, and I think he was calling them by their shorter names. I am certain that he said he had been moving in worlds not realised, and that they had shown him the Empire in a new light.

Still sore at recent neglect, I answered shortly, "Thank Heaven we have within the land ten thousand as good as they," and when he departed, asked him what he thought of things generally.

He replied with another quotation, to the effect that though singing was a remarkably fine performance, I was to be quite sure that few lips would be moved to song if they could find a sufficiency of kissing.

Whereby I understood that Eustace Cleever, decorator and colourman in words, was blaspheming his own Art, and would be sorry for this in the morning.

Milton Keynes UK
Ingram Content Group UK Ltd.
UKHW010707240424
441619UK00004B/344

9 789357 963343